Penguin Crime Fiction
Editor: Julian Symons
The Sailors' Rendezvous

Georges Simenon was born at Liège in Belgium in
1903. At sixteen he began work as a journalist on
the *Gazette de Liège*. He has published over 180
novels, in his own name, seventy of which belong
to the Inspector Maigret series, and his work has
been published in thirty-two languages. He has
had a great influence upon French cinema, and
more than forty of his novels have been filmed.

Simenon's novels are largely psychological. He
describes hidden fears, tensions and alliances
beneath the surface of life's ordinary routine, which
suddenly explode into violence and crime. André
Gide wrote to him: 'You are living on a false
reputation – just like Baudelaire or Chopin. But
nothing is more difficult than making the public go
back on a too hasty first impression. You are still
the slave of your first successes and the reader's
idleness would like to put a stop to your
triumphs there. . . . You are much more important
than is commonly supposed', and François Mauriac
wrote, 'I am afraid I may not have the courage
to descend right to the depths of this nightmare
which Simenon describes with such unendurable
art.'

Simenon has travelled a great deal and once lived
on a cutter, making long journeys of exploration
round the coasts of Northern Europe. He is
married and has four children, and lives near
Lausanne in Switzerland. He enjoys riding, fishing
and golf.

Georges Simenon

The Sailors' Rendezvous
A Maigret Mystery

Translated from the French by
Margaret Ludwig

Penguin Books

Penguin Books Ltd, Harmondsworth,
Middlesex, England
Penguin Books Inc, 7110 Ambassador Road,
Baltimore, Maryland 21207, U.S.A.
Penguin Books Australia Ltd, Ringwood,
Victoria, Australia
Penguin Books Canada Ltd, 41 Steelcase Road West,
Markham, Ontario, Canada
Penguin Books (N.Z.) Ltd, 182–190 Wairau Road,
Auckland 10, New Zealand

First published in Great Britain by Routledge in
Maigret Keeps a Rendezvous, 1940
Published in Penguin Books 1970
Reprinted 1972, 1975, 1976

Made and printed in Great Britain by
C. Nicholls & Company Ltd
Set in Linotype Times

This book is sold subject to the condition that
it shall not, by way of trade or otherwise, be lent,
re-sold, hired out, or otherwise circulated without
the publisher's prior consent in any form of
binding or cover other than that in which it is
published and without a similar condition
including this condition being imposed on the
subsequent purchaser

1. The Man Who Ate Glass

'He's the best lad in the place, and the mother, who has no one but him, may die of it. I am certain, as everyone is here, that he is innocent. But the sailors I've talked to say that he will be condemned, because Civil Courts have never understood anything about sea affairs. Do all you can, as if it were for me. I read in the papers that you have become a big noise in the *Police Judiciaire*, and . . .'

It was a morning in June. The windows were all open in the flat on the Boulevard Richard-Lenoir, and Madame Maigret was finishing packing some big basket-trunks while Maigret, collarless, was reading the letter half-aloud.

'Who's it from?'

'Jorissen. We were at school together. He became a teacher at Quimper. Tell me, are you very keen on spending our week's holiday in Alsace?'

She looked at him without understanding, the question was so unexpected. For twenty years they had invariably spent their holidays with relations in the same village in the east.

'Suppose we went to the sea instead?'

He re-read half-aloud some passages from the letter:

'You are in a better position than I am for getting accurate information. Briefly, Pierre Le Clinche, a young man of twenty who was a pupil of mine, sailed three months ago on the *Océan*, a Fécamp trawler which fishes cod in Newfoundland. The boat came back to port the day before yesterday. A few hours later, the captain's

5

body was found in the dock, and all the evidence points to murder. Now Pierre Le Clinche has been arrested . . .'

'Fécamp would be no worse for a holiday than anywhere else,' sighed Maigret, without enthusiasm.

But there was opposition. Madame Maigret was at home in Alsace, she helped with the jam and the plum-wine. The idea of living in a hotel in the company of other Parisians scared her.

'What shall I do all day?'

In the end she took some sewing and crochet-work.

'Well, don't ask me to bathe. I warn you of that now.'

*

They arrived at the *Hôtel de la Plage* at five o'clock, and Madame Maigret immediately began rearranging their room to her taste. Then they dined.

And now Maigret, all alone, was pushing open the frosted glass door of a harbour café, *Au Rendez-Vous des Terre-Neuvas*.

Just opposite, the trawler *Océan* was moored to the quay near a line of trucks. Acetylene lamps hung from the rigging, and in the harsh light people were moving about unloading the cod, which was passed from hand to hand and piled up in the trucks after being weighed.

There were ten of them working there, men and women, dirty, ragged, saturated with salt. And in front of the weighing-machine, a very clean young man, with a sea-cap over one ear and a note-book in his hand, was checking the weights. A rank, nauseating smell, which did not get less as you went away from it, and which the heat made heavier still, seeped into the bar.

Maigret sat down on a bench in an empty corner. The atmosphere around him was one of hubbub and excitement. The bar was full of sailors, some standing, others sitting, with their glasses on the marble tables.

'What will you have?'

6

'Beer.'

The proprietor came up after the barmaid.

'You know, I've another room across there for visitors. Here *they* make such a noise . . .'

He gave a wink.

'After three months at sea one can understand, eh?'

'They're the crew of the *Océan*?'

'Most of them. . . . The other boats haven't come back yet. . . . You mustn't mind them. There are some chaps who haven't been sober for three days. Are you staying here? You're a painter, I bet. . . . They come every now and again and sketch. Look! One of them did my head there, above the cash-desk.'

But the inspector gave so little encouragement to his chatter that he went off, quite put out.

'A copper! Who has a copper coin?' cried a sailor who was hardly as tall or as broad as a boy of sixteen. He had a grizzled head, with irregular features. Some of his teeth were missing. Drink had made his eyes shine, and he had a three days' growth of beard on his cheeks.

Someone gave him a copper. He bent it with his fingers, then put it between his teeth and snapped it in two.

'Whose turn next?'

He was showing off. He felt that he had caught the general attention, and was ready to do anything to hold it.

A bloated-looking engineer seized a coin, but he interrupted him:

'Wait! Here's something else you must do.'

He picked up an empty glass, took a big bite out of it and chewed up the bits, with every sign of satisfaction.

'Ha! ha! You might be able to do that some day. . . . More drinks, Léon!'

His glance roved round the room, like a second-rate actor's, and stopped at Maigret. He frowned. For a moment he was taken aback. Then he came forward, but he was so drunk that he had to support himself on the table.

'Come for me?' he said with a swagger.

'Steady, P'tit Louis!'

'Still the business of the pocket-book? Listen, you guys! ... You wouldn't believe me just now when I told you those stories about the Rue de Lappe.... Well, here's a big noise from the police going out of his way just because of this baby.... Will you let me have another drink?'

Now all eyes were on Maigret.

'Sit down here, P'tit Louis! Don't be a fool!'

But it was too much for P'tit Louis.

'You offer me a drink! No! It's not possible! What do you think, boys? The inspector is offering me a drink! ... A double dram, Léon!'

'You were on the *Océan*?'

This was another matter. P'tit Louis's face grew so dark that it seemed as if his drunkenness had vanished. He withdrew a little, defiantly, along the bench.

'So what?'

'Nothing.... Your health! ... How long have you been on the binge?'

'We've been at it for three days. Since we came ashore, you know. I gave Léon my money ... over nine hundred francs.... I hope there's some left! ... How much have I still got, Léon, you old cheat?'

'Certainly not enough to go on paying for drinks all round until morning. About fifty francs. Isn't it a shame, Inspector? Tomorrow he won't have a sou left, and he will have to sail on any old boat as a bunker-hand.... And it's the same every time. Not that I press them to drink. On the contrary ...'

'Shut up!'

The others had become dispirited. They talked in low tones, and kept turning towards the inspector's table.

'They're all from the *Océan*?'

'Except the big chap in the cap, who is a pilot, and the red-haired one, who is a ship's carpenter ...'

'Tell me what happened.'

'I've nothing to say.'

'Listen, P'tit Louis! Don't forget the pocket-book business when you are doing your glass-eating act in the Bastille.'

'I won't get more than three months for it, and I'm just needing a rest. If you feel like that, we can go at once.'

'You worked in the engine-room?'

'Of course. As usual, I was second stoker.'

'You saw the captain often?'

'Perhaps twice altogether.'

'And the radio operator?'

'Don't know!'

'Léon, fill up the glasses.'

P'tit Louis gave a contemptuous laugh.

'I could drink until I burst and still I would only say what I wanted to. But while you're at it you might offer the boys a drink. After a foul trip like that ...'

A sailor who couldn't have been twenty edged up and pulled at P'tit Louis's sleeve. Then they both began talking in Breton.

'What's he saying?'

'That it's time I went to bed.'

'Is he your friend?'

P'tit Louis shrugged his shoulders, and as the other tried to take his glass from him he emptied it defiantly at one gulp.

The Breton had thick eyebrows and wavy hair.

'Sit down beside us,' said Maigret.

But the sailor went off without answering, and sat down at another table, where he continued to stare fixedly at the two men.

The atmosphere was heavy and salt-laden. You could

9

hear the voices of the summer visitors, playing dominoes in the next room, where it was cleaner and airier.

'Much cod?' asked Maigret, who followed up an idea with the relentlessness of an electric drill.

'Filth! It arrived half-rotten.'

'Why was that?'

'Not salted enough. . . . Or too much! . . . What muck! Not a third of the men will sail next week . . .'

'You're off again?'

'*Parbleu!* What are engines for? Sailing-ships make only one trip, from February to September. But trawlers have time to go twice to the Banks.'

'Will you go back?'

P'tit Louis spat on the ground and shrugged wearily.

'I'd sooner go to Fresnes. . . . A lousy business! . . .'

'The captain?'

'I've nothing to say.'

He had picked up the butt-end of a cigar and lit it. Suddenly he rushed into the street, where they saw him vomiting, standing on the edge of the pavement, where the Breton joined him.

'Poor devil!' sighed the proprietor. 'The day before yesterday he had nearly a thousand francs in his pocket. Today it's a near thing if he doesn't owe me money. Oysters and lobster! Without reckoning that he pays for drinks for everyone as if he didn't know what to do with his money.'

'You knew the radio operator on the *Océan*?'

'He lodged here. Look! He used to feed at that table, then he would go and write in the other room to have more peace.'

'Whom did he write to?'

'It wasn't only letters. Poetry or novels, as you might say. He was an educated, well-mannered boy. Now that I know you're from the police I can tell you they've made a great mistake.'

'It doesn't alter the fact that the captain was killed!'

A shrug of the shoulders. The proprietor sat down in front of Maigret. P'tit Louis came in, made for the counter and ordered a drink. And his companion went on urging him in Breton to keep quiet.

'You mustn't pay any attention. Once they're ashore they're always like this, drinking, shouting, fighting, breaking windows. On board ship they work like demons. Yes, even P'tit Louis. . . . The chief engineer of the *Océan* told me only yesterday that he does the work of two men. . . At sea a boiler feed-pipe exploded. . . . It was dangerous to repair. . . . Nobody wanted to go. . . . It was P'tit Louis who took it on. . . . Once they stop drinking . . .'

Léon lowered his voice and looked mistrustfully at his customers.

'This time they've maybe got other reasons for putting away their liquor. They won't tell you anything because you're not from the sea. . . . But I hear them talking. . . . I'm an old pilot. . . . There are things . . .'

'Things?'

'It's difficult to explain. . . . You know there aren't enough fishers in Fécamp for all the trawlers. . . . They get them from Brittany. . . . These chaps have queer ideas, and they're superstitious . . .'

He lowered his voice until it was scarcely audible.

'It seems that this time it was the evil eye. It began even in port when they were getting off. A sailor climbed up a derrick to wave to his wife. He was holding on to a rope and it broke, and there he was on the deck with his leg smashed. They had to take him ashore in a dinghy. . . . And there was a cabin-boy who didn't want to go, and howled and wept! Well, three days later there was a wireless message to say that he'd been swept overboard by a wave! A kid of fifteen . . . a little thin fair-haired kid with a name like a girl's . . . Jean-Marie. . . . And then

11

... Give us some Calvados, Julie. The bottle on the right.
... No! not that one ... the one with the glass stopper ...'

'The evil eye went on working?'

'I don't know anything definitely. You'd think they were all afraid to speak. All the same, if the radio operator was arrested it was because the police had heard that he and the captain hadn't spoken a word the whole trip. ... They were like cat and dog!'

'And then what? ...'

'Things ... things that meant nothing.... Listen! The captain made them take the boat to a part where no cod had ever been seen. And he roared at them because the head-fisher refused to obey! He took out his revolver ... they were mad about it! They didn't take a ton in a whole month. Then suddenly the fishing became good.... All the same, the cod had to be sold at half-price because it was badly salted. Everything! Even coming into port they made two false manoeuvres, and sank a boat. As if they'd had a curse on them! ... The captain sent everyone on shore that evening, without leaving anyone on guard, and stayed on board himself all alone.

'It must have been about nine o'clock. They were all here getting tight. The radio operator had gone up to his room. Then he went out.... He was seen going towards the boat ...

'It was then that it happened.... A fisher who was getting ready to go out at the lower end of the harbour, heard the sound of something falling into the water ...

'He ran up with a customs man he met on the way. They lit lanterns. There was a body in the dock, caught on the chain of the *Océan*'s anchor.

'It was the captain.... They got him out dead.... They applied artificial respiration. They couldn't make it out, because he'd only been ten minutes in the water ...

'It was the doctor who explained.... It seems he'd

been strangled beforehand. D'you see? . . . And they found the operator in his cabin, which is behind the funnel – you can see it from here. . . . The police came here to search his room, and found his papers burnt . . .

'What do you make of it? . . . Two Calvados, Julie! . . . Your health!'

P'tit Louis, who was getting more and more worked up, seized a chair between his teeth and, in the middle of a circle of sailors, raised it horizontally with a defiant look at Maigret.

'The captain is from these parts?' asked the inspector.

'Yes! A queer chap! Scarcely bigger or broader than P'tit Louis. And always polite and pleasant. And as neat as a new pin! I don't think he's ever been seen in the café. He wasn't married. But he lodged with a widow, the wife of a customs official, in Rue d'Etretat. They used to say he'd end up by marrying her. He'd been going to Newfoundland for fifteen years . . . always for the same firm: *La Morue Française*. Captain Fallut, that was his name. They're in a bit of a jam about sending the *Océan* back to the Bank. No Captain! And half the crew not wanting to sign on again . . .'

'Why?'

'You mustn't look for reasons. It's the evil eye, as I've told you. They're considering laying up the boat until next year. Apart from the fact that the police have asked the crew to hold themselves at their disposal . . .'

'Is the radio operator in prison?'

'Yes; they took him off that evening, bracelets and all. I was at the door, and I don't mind telling you my wife cried about it . . . and I myself. And yet he wasn't a particularly good customer. I gave him special prices . . . and he hardly drank anything . . .'

They were interrupted by a sudden uproar. P'tit Louis had fallen on the Breton, probably because he insisted on keeping him from drinking. They were both rolling on the ground. The others were getting out of the way.

It was Maigret who separated them by literally hauling them up, one with each hand.

'Well . . . do you want to bite each other's noses off?'

The whole thing happened quickly. The Breton, who had his hands free, drew a knife from his pocket, and the inspector saw it just in time to kick it spinning two yards with a movement of his heel. His boot hit the Breton on the chin, which began to bleed. And then P'tit Louis threw himself on his companion, still in a drunken daze, and began to cry and beg his pardon.

Léon came up to Maigret, watch in hand:

'It's closing time. Otherwise we'll have the police here. Every evening it's the same story. Impossible to get them out . . .'

'Do they sleep on board the *Océan*?'

'Yes. Except when, as happened yesterday with two of them, they stay in the gutter. I found them there this morning when I opened the shutters . . .'

The barmaid was collecting the glasses off the tables. The men went out in threes and fours. Only P'tit Louis and the Breton made no move.

'D'you want a room?' Léon asked Maigret.

'Thank you! I'm putting up at the *Hôtel de la Plage*!'

'I say . . .'

'What?'

'It's not that I want to interfere. It's none of my business. Only we were fond of that operator. Perhaps it wouldn't be a bad idea to *cherchez la femme*, as they say in novels. I've heard whispers . . .'

'Had Pierre Le Clinche a mistress?'

'Him? Oh, no. . . . He was engaged to a girl in his own part of the country, and every day he used to send a six-page letter to her . . .'

'Then who . . .?'

'I don't know at all. Perhaps it's more complicated than one thinks. And then . . .'

'And then . . . ?'

'Nothing! . . . Be sensible, P'tit Louis! Go to bed . . .'

But P'tit Louis was in an advanced state of drunkenness. He was maudlin. He embraced his comrade, whose chin was still bleeding, and begged for forgiveness.

Maigret went out, his hands in his pockets, his coat-collar turned up, for the air was chilly.

In the entrance hall of the *Hôtel de la Plage* he saw a girl sitting in a basket-chair. A man rose from another chair and smiled with a trace of embarrassment.

It was Jorissen, the teacher from Quimper. Maigret hadn't seen him for fifteen years, and the teacher wasn't quite sure how to address him.

'Excuse . . . excuse me. I . . . we've just arrived, Mademoiselle Léonnec and I. . . . I looked in all the hotels. They said that you . . . that you'd be back. This is Pierre Le Clinche's fiancée. She absolutely insisted . . .'

A tall, rather pale girl, a little timid. But when Maigret shook hands with her, he realized that behind her provincial awkwardness and coquetry there was a will.

She said nothing. She was too impressed. So was Jorissen, the simple teacher, who found his old comrade one of the big noises of the *Police Judiciaire*.

'Madame Maigret was just pointed out to me in the drawing-room. . . . I didn't dare . . .'

Maigret looked at the girl. She was neither pretty nor plain, but her simplicity was rather touching.

'You know he's innocent, don't you?' she managed to say without looking at anyone.

The porter was waiting to get back to his bed. He had already unbuttoned his waistcoat.

'We'll see about that tomorrow. You've got a room? . . .'

'The room next to yours, Maig – Inspector,' the

teacher from Quimper stammered in confusion. 'And Mademoiselle Léonnec is on the floor above. I'm afraid I'll have to go back tomorrow on account of examinations. . . . Do you think . . . ?'

'Tomorrow! We'll see!' Maigret repeated.

As he was getting into bed, his wife murmured, half-asleep: 'Don't forget to turn the light out.'

2. The Yellow Shoes

They walked side by side without looking at each other, first along the beach, which was deserted at that hour, then along the quays.

And gradually the silences became rarer. Marie Léonnec managed to talk in an almost natural voice.

'You'll find that you'll like him straight away! You couldn't do anything else. And then you'll understand that . . .'

Maigret stole curious and admiring glances at her. Jorissen had gone back to Quimper in the early morning, leaving the girl alone at Fécamp.

'I don't insist on her coming back with me. She has a will of her own!' he had said.

The evening before, she had been as negative as a girl brought up in the calm of a little town can be. But in less than an hour after Jorissen's departure they were leaving the *Hôtel de la Plage*, she and Maigret.

Maigret wore his most forbidding look. But she just wasn't impressed, refused to notice it, and smiled confidently.

'His only fault,' she went on, 'is that he is extremely sensitive. But how should he be anything else? His father was only a fisher. His mother mended nets for a long time so that he could be educated. Now it is he who supports her. He is educated. He has a fine future before him . . .'

'Are your parents well off?' Maigret asked bluntly.

'They are the biggest makers of nets and metal cables in Quimper. That's why Pierre didn't even want to speak to my father. For a whole year we met secretly . . .'

'You were both eighteen?'

'More or less. . . . It was I who told my family. And Pierre swore he would only marry me when he was earning at least two thousand francs a month. You see . . .'

'Has he written to you since he was arrested?'

'Only one letter. A very short one! And he who used to write pages and pages every day! He said it would be better for me and my parents that I should announce in the district that everything had been broken off.'

They passed the *Océan*, which was still being unloaded. At high tide her black hull dominated the wharf. On the fo'c's'le deck three men, bare to the waist, were washing themselves. Among them Maigret recognized P'tit Louis.

His eye caught a movement: one of the sailors nudged his companion and pointed at Maigret and the girl. Maigret frowned.

'That's considerate, isn't it?' went on the voice beside him. 'He knows what proportions a scandal assumes in a small town like Quimper. He wanted to give me back my freedom.'

It was a clear morning. The girl in her grey tailored suit could have been a student or a teacher.

'It shows that my parents must have confidence in him too, for them to have let me come! And yet my father would prefer to see me married to a commercial traveller . . .'

Maigret made her stay for a while in the waiting-room of the police station while he made some notes.

Half an hour later they both went into the prison.

*

It was a very grumpy Maigret who stood with hunched shoulders, his hands behind his back, his pipe gripped between his teeth, in a corner of the cell. He had told the authorities that he was not working on the case in any official capacity, but was only following it out of curiosity.

Several people had described the radio operator to him, and the mental image he had made corresponded in every detail to the lad before him.

A tall, thin young man in a crumpled but correct suit, his face at once serious and timid, like a boy who is top of the class. Clusters of freckles under his eyes, and hair cropped short like stubble.

He jumped up when the door opened, and for a long moment he held back from the girl as she came towards him. She had literally to throw herself into his arms and remain there by force while he cast distracted looks all round.

'Marie! . . . Who's that? . . . How . . .?'

He was in a highly nervous state, but made every effort to conceal it. Only his spectacles were rather moist and his lip trembled.

'You shouldn't have come . . .'

He looked at the unknown figure of Maigret, and then at the door, which had been left ajar.

He had no collar on and no shoelaces, but a reddish beard of several days' growth. Desperate as was his situation, all this troubled him. He fingered his bare neck and prominent Adam's apple with embarrassment.

'Does my mother . . .?'

'She hasn't come! But she doesn't believe either that you're guilty.'

Even the girl couldn't give free vent to her emotion. It was like a scene that hadn't come off, perhaps because the atmosphere was too crude.

They looked at each other and didn't know what to

18

say, tried to find words. Then Marie Léonnec pointed to Maigret.

'This is a friend of Jorissen's. He's an inspector in the *Police Judiciaire*, and he's said he'll help us . . .'

Le Clinche started to hold out his hand but didn't dare.

'Thank you. . . . I . . .'

It was a mix-up all along the line, and the girl, realizing it, wanted to cry. She had counted on a moving interview that would convince Maigret.

She looked at her fiancé with vexation, with even a touch of impatience.

'You must say everything you can that will help in your defence.'

Pierre Le Clinche sighed, awkward and bored.

'I've only a few questions to ask you,' put in the inspector. 'All the crew is agreed in saying that during the course of the trip your relations with the captain were cold, to say the least of it. Now, when you went off you were on rather good terms. What caused the change?'

The operator opened his mouth, said nothing, and fixed a desolate eye on the floor.

'Was it a matter of routine? The first two days you fed with the second officer and the chief engineer. After that you preferred to eat with the men . . .'

'Yes . . . I know . . .'

'Why?'

And Marie Léonnec cried impatiently:

'Do talk, Pierre! It's to get you off! You must tell us the truth.'

'I don't know . . .'

He seemed without any feelings or incentive, almost without hope.

'Did you have any arguments with Captain Fallut?'

'No . . .'

'Yet you lived for nearly three months on the same boat without saying a word to him. Everyone noticed it.

There are rumours that at certain times Fallut gave the impression that he'd gone mad . . .'

'I don't know . . .'

Marie Léonnec tried to keep from sobbing under the nervous strain.

'When the *Océan* came into port, you went ashore with the others. In your hotel room you burned some papers . . .'

'Yes. That was of no importance . . .'

'You have a habit of keeping a diary of everything you see. Wasn't it the diary of this trip that you burned?'

He stood there hanging his head like a schoolboy who hasn't learned the lesson and stares fixedly at the ground.

'Yes . . .'

'Why?'

'I don't know now.'

'And you don't know why you went back on board? But not straight away! . . . You were seen hiding behind a truck fifty yards from the boat . . .'

The girl looked at the inspector, then at her fiancé, then back again at the inspector. This was beginning to be beyond her.

'Yes . . .'

'The captain came down the gangway and set foot on the quay. It was at that moment that he was attacked . . .'

He still said nothing.

'Damn it, man, can't you answer?'

'Yes, answer, Pierre! It's to get you free. I don't understand. . . . I . . .'

Tears welled up in her eyes.

'Yes . . .'

'Yes what?'

'I was there!'

'Well, then, did you see? . . .'

'Not very well. . . . There was a pile of barrels, and some trucks. There was a struggle between two men, then one of them ran off and a body fell into the water . . .'

'What did the man who ran away look like?'

'I don't know.'

'Was he in sailor's clothes?'

'No.'

'Well, then, you know how he was dressed?'

'I only noticed his yellow shoes when he was passing near a gas-light . . .'

'What did you do next?'

'I went on board . . .'

'Why? And why didn't you get help for the captain? Did you know he was already dead? . . .'

A heavy silence. Marie Léonnec clasped her hands in anguish.

'Speak, Pierre! Speak, I beg you!'

'Yes. . . . No. . . . I swear I don't know!'

There were steps in the corridor. The gaoler had come to say that the examining magistrate was waiting for Le Clinche.

His fiancée wanted to kiss him. He hung back. Finally he took her slowly in his arms with an absent-minded expression.

And he did not kiss her mouth, but the delicate little curls on her temples.

'Pierre! . . .'

'You shouldn't have come!' he said, his brow furrowed, and followed the gaoler with a weary step.

Maigret and Marie Léonnec got outside without saying anything. Then she sighed with an effort:

'I don't understand. . . . I . . .'

Then, straightening her head:

'But he's innocent, all the same, I'm sure! We don't understand, because we've never been in such a situation. For three days now he's been in prison, with everybody accusing him. . . . And he's a timid man!'

Maigret was quite touched by the way she did her best to put energy into her words, although she was quite discouraged.

'You'll do something, all the same, won't you?'

'On condition that you go back home to Quimper ...'

'No! ... Not that! Listen. ... Let me ...'

'Well, go down to the beach and sit with my wife and try to do something. She'll probably have some embroidery for you ...'

'What are you going to do? Do you think that the clue of the yellow shoes ...?'

People looked back at them because Marie Léonnec was so animated that it looked as if they were quarrelling.

'I repeat that I'll do everything that's in my power. ... Listen! This street leads straight to the *Hôtel de la Plage*. Tell my wife that I'll perhaps be a bit late for lunch ...'

And he turned and went down to the quay.

His irritated look was gone. He was almost smiling.

He had feared an emotional scene in the cell, with vehement protestations, tears and kisses. But it had gone off quite differently, it had been simpler, and at the same time more heart-rending and significant.

The man's personality pleased him, just because there was something distant and concentrated about it.

In front of a shop he met P'tit Louis with a pair of rubber boots in his hand.

'Where are you going?'

'To sell them! Like to buy them? They make much better ones in Canada. I bet you won't find the like of this in France. Two hundred francs ...'

All the same, P'tit Louis was a little uncomfortable and was only waiting to be allowed to go on his way.

'Has it ever occurred to you that Captain Fallut was a bit touched?'

'You don't see much in the bunkers, you know ...'

'But you hear things.... Well?'

'Of course there were some funny stories! ...'

'What?'

'All kinds.... Nothing! ... It's difficult to explain. ... Especially once you're on shore!'

He still had his boots in his hand, and the ship-chandler, who had spotted him, was waiting at his door.

'Do you need me any longer?'

'When exactly did it begin?'

'Straight away.... A boat is either lucky or unlucky! The *Océan* was unlucky ...'

'Bad seamanship?'

'That among other things! What do you expect me to say? ... Things that don't make sense, but are there all the same.... The proof is that there was a feeling we wouldn't come back.... I say, is it true that I'm not going to be bothered about that pocket-book any more?'

'We'll see ...'

The harbour was almost empty. In summer all the ships were away in Newfoundland except the fishing-boats that catch fresh fish along the coast. There was only the gaunt profile of the *Océan* in the dock, and from there came the strong smell of cod which filled the air.

Near the trucks was a man in leather gaiters and a braided cap.

'Is that the owner?' Maigret asked a customs man who was passing.

'Yes – that's the director of *La Morue Française* ...'

The inspector introduced himself. The director gave him a suspicious look without interrupting his work of overseeing the unloading.

'What do you think about the murder of your captain?'

'What do I think? I think that here's eight hundred

tons of damaged cod. And that if it goes on like this, the boat won't make a second trip. And it's not the police who settle up these matters or meet the deficit!'

'You had complete trust in Fallut, then?'

'Yes! ... What next?'

'You think it was the operator? ...'

'Operator or not, it's a wasted year. Not to mention the state the nets were in when they brought them back! Nets that cost two million francs, d'you hear? Torn as if they'd amused themselves fishing from the rocks. ... And on top of that, a crew that talks about the evil eye. ... Hi! down there. ... What the hell are you doing? ... Did I say, yes or no, that this truck was to be loaded before anything else? ...'

And he began running along the boat, fulminating against the whole world.

Maigret stayed a few minutes watching the unloading. Then he went off in the direction of the jetty, among the fishers in their blouses of rust-coloured sailcloth.

Before long he heard a voice behind him:

'Sst! Sst! ... Inspector! Inspector!'

It was Léon, the proprietor of the *Rendez-Vous des Terre-Neuvas*, who was trying to catch up with him as fast as his little legs would carry him.

'Come and have something on the house ...'

He wore a mysterious look, which seemed to promise all manner of things. On the way he explained.

'Things are quieting down! Those who haven't gone home to Brittany or their own villages have spent nearly all their money. ... This morning I'd only some mackerel fishers ...'

They crossed the quay and entered the café, which was empty, except for the barmaid who was wiping the tables.

'Wait. ... What'll you have? ... A small *apéritif*. It's nearly time for one. You see, as I told you yesterday,

I don't press people to drink. On the contrary! And above all, when they've finished I don't charge them for more than what they owe me. Go and see whether I'm wanted in the kitchen, Julie! . . .'

He gave the inspector a knowing wink.

'Your health! . . . I saw you a long way off. So, as I'd something to tell you . . .'

He went to make sure that the girl wasn't listening behind the door. Then, with an increasingly enigmatic but delighted look, he drew something out of his pocket, a piece of cardboard the shape of a photograph.

"*Voilà!* What do you say to that?'

It was a photograph all right, the photograph of a woman. But the head was scribbled all over with red ink. A furious attempt had been made to eradicate the face completely. The pen had scratched holes in the paper. There were lines in every direction so that not a square millimetre was left visible.

Below the head, however, the bust was left untouched. The bosom was opulent, the dress made of some shiny satin, very tight and low-cut.

'Where did you find this?'

More winks . . .

'I don't mind telling you, as we're alone. Le Clinche's locker shuts rather badly. So he had the habit of slipping his fiancée's letters under his table-cloth.'

'And you used to read them?'

'Oh, they were quite uninteresting. It was only by chance. . . . When they made a search they didn't think of looking under the cover. . . . The idea occurred to me in the evening, and this is what I found. Of course you can't see the head. But it's not the fiancée. She's not that build. I've seen her portrait too. So there is another woman in the background . . .'

Maigret looked intently at the portrait. The line of the shoulders was alluring. The woman must be rather older

25

than Marie Léonnec. There was something extremely sensual about the bust.

A bit vulgar, too! The dress looked like a cheap copy of some fancy model.

'Is there any red ink in the place?'

'No! Nothing but green ink.'

'Le Clinche never used red ink?'

'Never. . . . He had his own ink for his fountain-pen. Special ink, blue-black.'

Maigret rose and made for the door.

'You'll excuse me?'

A few minutes later he was on board the *Océan* rummaging in the operator's cabin, then in the captain's, which was dirty and disorderly.

There was no red ink on board, and the fishers had never seen any.

As he left the ship Maigret got a dirty look from the owner, who was still vituperating against the world.

'Is there any red ink in your offices?'

'Red ink? What for? We don't keep a school . . .'

But, as if he remembered something, he added brusquely:

'Fallut was the only one who used red ink when he was at home in the Rue d'Etretat. Is it still this same story? . . . Mind the truck down there! . . . It just needs an accident. . . . Well, what do you want with your red ink? . . .'

'Nothing! . . . Thank you . . .'

P'tit Louis was coming back without his boots but with a pair of spectacles on his nose, a cadet's cap on his head, and old down-at-heel shoes on his feet.

3. The Portrait Without a Head

'Which could not be said of me in any circumstances, as I have savings which are quite equal to a captain's pay...'

Maigret left Madame Bernard on the doorstep of her little house in the Rue d'Etretat. She was a well-preserved woman in her fifties, and she had just talked for a solid half-hour about her first husband, her widowhood, the captain who had been her boarder, the rumours that had gone round about their relationship, and finally about the unknown who was certainly a 'loose-living woman'.

The inspector had been shown round the whole house, which was well kept but full of objects in bad taste. Captain Fallut's room was still as it had been arranged in preparation for his return.

Few personal possessions: some clothes in a trunk, some books – mostly adventure novels, and photographs of boats.

It all gave the impression of a placid, mediocre existence.

'There was no contract, but we had an understanding, and everybody knew that we'd end up by getting married. I supplied the house, the furniture, and the linen. . . . Nothing would have been altered and we should have been quite comfortable, especially in three years when he'd have had his pension . . .'

From the windows one could see the grocer's opposite, the sloping street and the pavement where children were playing.

'Then last winter he met that woman and everything was upset. At his age, too! . . . Is it possible to get so infatuated about a creature like that? And he made such a mystery out of it. He must have gone to Le Havre or somewhere to see her, because they were never seen together. I felt there was something in the wind. He bought thinner underwear ... and even silk socks once! As there was nothing between us it was none of my business, and I didn't want to appear to be defending my own interests ...'

A whole side of the dead man's life was cleared up by this conversation with Madame Bernard. The little man, well on in years, who came back to port after a fishing trip and spent the winter living like a good bourgeois with Madame Bernard, who looked after him and waited for him to marry her.

He ate with her in the dining-room under the portrait of the first husband with the blond moustache. Then he would go to his room and read an adventure story.

And suddenly this peaceful existence was disturbed. Another woman appeared. Captain Fallut began to frequent Le Havre, to dress better and to shave more closely, even bought silk socks and hid from his landlady.

But he wasn't married or engaged. He was free, yet he never once showed himself at Fécamp with the stranger.

Was it *la grande passion*, life's great adventure arriving rather late? Or merely a sordid affair?

*

Maigret arrived at the beach and saw his wife sitting on a red-striped deck-chair, and beside her Marie Léonnec sewing.

Some people were bathing on the beach, which was white in the sun. A lazy sea. And over there on the other side of the jetty, the *Océan* lay in the dock, with her cargo of cod still in process of being unloaded, and her sullen crew talking in phrases full of hidden meaning.

He kissed Madame Maigret on the forehead and bowed to the girl, answering her inquiring eyes with a 'Nothing special'.

His wife said in a placid voice:

'Mademoiselle Léonnec has told me her whole story. Do you think the boy is capable of doing such a thing?'

They went slowly back to the hotel, Maigret carrying the two folded deck-chairs. Just as they were sitting down at table a policeman in uniform came up looking for the inspector.

'I was told to show you this. It came in an hour ago . . .'

And he held out a yellow envelope which had been opened and had no address. Inside was a sheet of paper with cramped, precise handwriting:

No one is to be accused of my death, and do not seek to understand my action.

These are my last wishes. I leave all that I possess to the widow Bernard who has always been good to me, and I charge her to send my gold chronometer to my nephew and to see that I am buried in the cemetery at Fécamp beside my mother . . .

Maigret opened his eyes wide.

'It's signed Octave Fallut,' he said softly. 'How did this letter come to the police station?'

'We don't know. It was found in the letter-box. The signature seems to be quite genuine. The superintendent immediately informed the public prosecutor . . .'

'But that doesn't alter the fact that he was strangled! And that it is impossible to strangle yourself!' growled Maigret.

Beside them the table d'hôte was clamouring to be eaten. There were red radishes on a dish.

'Wait a moment while I copy this letter. Because I expect you ought to take it back?'

'I haven't any special instructions, but I suppose ...'

'Yes, it ought to be kept in the dossier.'

A little later, Maigret, his copy in his hand, looked impatiently round the dining-room where he would have to waste an hour waiting for the various dishes. All this time Marie Léonnec hadn't taken her eyes off his face, but she had not dared to interrupt his sulky meditation. Only Madame Maigret, confronted with pale veal cutlets, sighed:

'All the same, we would have been better off in Alsace ...'

Maigret rose before dessert, and wiped his mouth, in a hurry to see the ship, the harbour, and the sailors again. On the way he muttered:

'Fallut knew he was going to die! But did he know that he was going to be killed? Did he want to save his murderer in advance, or did he just want to commit suicide?

'Besides, who put the yellow envelope into the letter-box? It was neither stamped nor addressed.'

The news had already gone round, for, when Maigret got near the ship, the director of *La Morue Française* called out with aggressive irony:

'Well, it seems that Fallut strangled himself! Who found that out?'

'I'd rather you'd tell me which of the officers of the *Océan* are still on board?'

'None of them! The second officer has gone off on a bust to Paris. The chief engineer is at his home at Yport and won't be back until the unloading is finished.'

Maigret went back again into the captain's cabin. A narrow cabin. A bed with a dirty counterpane. A cupboard in the bulkhead. A blue enamel coffee-pot on a table covered with oilcloth. Boots with wooden soles in the corner.

It was gloomy and pitchy, saturated with the acrid

smell that reigned over the entire ship. Striped blue jerseys were drying on the bridge. Maigret nearly slipped as he crossed the gangway, which was greasy with fishes' entrails.

'Have you found anything?'

The inspector shrugged his shoulders, looked back again lugubriously at the *Océan*, and asked a customs man how one could get to Yport.

Yport was a village at the foot of the cliffs, six kilometres from Fécamp. A few fishermen's cottages. A few farms scattered around about. Some villas, mostly let furnished during the summer season, and a single hotel.

On the beach more bathers, children, and mammas with their knitting or embroidery.

'Monsieur Laberge's house, please?'

'The chief engineer of the *Océan* or the farmer?'

'The chief engineer.'

He was shown a little house surrounded by a small garden. And as he approached the green-painted gate, the sound of a dispute came to him from inside the house. Two voices, a man's and a woman's. But he couldn't make out the words, and he knocked.

There was a silence. Steps approached. The door opened and a tall thin man appeared, suspicious and surly.

'What is it?'

A woman in an overall quickly began to tidy her hair.

'I'm from the *Police Judiciaire*, and I should like to ask you some questions.'

'Come in.'

A little boy was crying, and his father pushed him savagely into the next room, where the end of a bed was visible.

'You can leave us!' said Laberge to his wife. Her eyes were red too. The quarrel must have broken out during the meal, for the plates were only half-empty.

'What do you want to know?'

'How long is it since you stopped going to Fécamp?'

'This morning. . . . I went there on my bike – it's not very amusing to hear the wife nagging at you the whole day. You spend months at sea until you could burst. And then when you get home . . .'

His anger had not subsided. To tell the truth, his breath reeked of alcohol.

'They're all the same. Jealousy and suspicion. They think your one idea is to go with tarts. Listen! There she is taking it out of the kid to soothe her nerves . . .'

The child was certainly crying in the next room, and they heard the woman's voice raised:

'Will you be quiet? Stop it, will you!'

The words must have been accompanied by slaps or blows, for the sobs broke out louder than ever.

'Oh! It's a fine life . . .'

'Did Captain Fallut ever involve you in any kind of trouble?'

The man looked queerly at Maigret and moved uneasily.

'What makes you think that?'

'Have you been sailing long with him?'

'Five years.'

'And on board you took your meals together.'

'Except this time! He took it into his head to eat alone in his cabin. But I'd much prefer not to talk about that foul trip!'

'Where were you when the crime was committed?'

'At the café with the others. They must have told you . . .'

'And you believe that the operator had a reason for attacking the captain?'

Laberge suddenly got angry.

'What are you getting at with your questions? What do you want me to say? I wasn't asked to be a police spy, d'you hear? I'm fed up! With this business and everything else! Up to the point when I wonder whether I'll sign on for the next trip!'

'Evidently the last one wasn't very brilliant!'

Another sharp look at Maigret.

'What do you mean?'

'That everything went wrong. A cabin-boy got killed. There were more accidents than usual. The fishing wasn't good, and the cod was damaged when it arrived at Fécamp.'

'Is it my fault?'

'I don't say that! I'm just asking whether you took part in any incident which might explain the death of the captain. He was a temperate man, leading an orderly life . . .'

The engineer sneered but said nothing.

'Did you ever know him to have an adventure?'

'I tell you I know nothing, and I'm fed to the teeth with the whole thing. Do you want to drive me mad? What do *you* want now? . . .'

It was his wife he was talking to. She had just come into the room and gone over to the stove where a pan was giving off a smell of burning.

She must have been about thirty-five, neither pretty nor ugly.

'One moment,' she said humbly. 'It's the dog's meat . . .'

'Hurry up! Isn't it ready yet?'

And to Maigret:

'Would you like me to give you a good tip? Leave all this alone! Fallut's all right where he is. And the less said about it the better. Now, I know nothing about it, and if you went on questioning me all night I wouldn't have another word to say. Did you come by train? If you don't take the one that goes in ten minutes you won't get another before eight o'clock in the evening . . .'

He had opened the door. Sunlight poured into the room.

'Whom is your wife jealous of?' the inspector asked softly, when he was on the doorstep.

Laberge clenched his teeth without saying a word.

'Do you know this person?'

And Maigret held out the portrait whose head had disappeared under the red-ink scribbles. But he held his thumb on the head. Only the satin corsage was visible.

Laberge cast a swift look at him and could hardly refrain from snatching the piece of cardboard.

'You recognize her?'

'How do you expect me to recognize her?'

And he again held out his hand, while Maigret put the portrait back in his pocket.

'You're coming to Fécamp tomorrow?'

'I don't know. . . . You want me?'

'No. I was just asking. Thank you for the information you were so good as to give me.'

'I haven't given you any information.'

Maigret had not gone ten steps when the door was kicked shut and the voices inside the house took up the quarrel again more fiercely than ever.

*

The chief engineer had told the truth: there wasn't another train back to Fécamp before eight in the evening, and Maigret, with nothing to do, was hopelessly stranded on the beach, where he established himself on the hotel terrace.

It had the commonplace atmosphere of holiday resorts: red sun-umbrellas, white dresses, flannel trousers, and a curious group round a fishing-boat which was being dragged up the beach by means of a windlass. White cliffs to left and right. In front the sea, pale green with a white fringe and the regular murmur of wavelets on the shore.

'Beer! . . .'

The sun was hot. A family was eating ices at the next table. A young man was taking snapshots with a kodak, and from somewhere came the shrill voices of girls.

Maigret let his glance wander round the scene. His thoughts strayed and his brain went into a torpid reverie of increasing inconsistency, revolving round Captain Fallut.

'Many thanks!'

These words were impressed in his mind, not because of their meaning but because of the way they were said, dryly, with bitter irony, by a woman behind him.

'But, as I've told you, Adèle . . .'

'Go to blazes!'

'You're not going to begin again?'

'I'll do what I like.'

It certainly was a day of quarrels! That morning Maigret had come across a very prickly fellow, the director of *La Morue Française*. At Yport there had been the domestic scene in the Laberges' home. And here on the terrace was an unknown couple exchanging decidedly sharp words.

'You'd better think it over.'

'Go to blazes!'

'You think it's intelligent to answer like that?'

'Go to hell! D'you understand? . . . Waiter, this lemonade is tepid! Go and get me another! . . .'

Her accent was vulgar and she talked louder than was necessary.

'All the same, you must decide . . .' the man went on.

'Go there all by myself? I've already told you! And leave me alone.'

'You know it's pretty mean, what you are doing.'

'What about you?'

'Me? You dare.... My hat! If we weren't here, I don't think I'd be able to restrain myself...'

She laughed. Far too loudly.

'Oh, go on, ducky!'

'Please be quiet!'

'And why should I be quiet?'

'Because!'

'I must say that's an intelligent answer...'

'Are you going to be quiet?'

'If I please...'

'Adèle, I warn you that...'

'That what?... Are you going to make a scene in front of everybody? Well, you're getting on.... People are listening already...'

'You'd better think it over, and then you'll see...'

She jumped up as if she'd had enough. Maigret had his back to her, but he saw her shadow lengthening on the flagstones of the terrace.

Then he saw her from behind, as she walked off towards the sea.

With the light behind her she was just a silhouette against a reddening sky. Maigret only noticed that she was well dressed, and that she was not in beach costume but wore silk stockings and high heels.

This made walking difficult and ungraceful for her when she got on the sand. Every moment she nearly sprained her ankle, but she kept on, angry and obstinate.

'What do I owe you, waiter?'

'But I haven't brought madame's lemonade yet...'

'Doesn't matter. How much is it?'

'Nine francs fifty. You're not dining here?...'

'I've no idea...'

Maigret turned to look at the man, who showed a certain embarrassment, for he knew that the people round about had heard everything.

He was tall, with a flashy kind of elegance. His eyes were tired and his whole face betrayed extreme mental exhaustion. He stood up, undecided what direction to take, then, assuming an air of indifference, walked towards the young woman who was now following the sinuous line of the sea.

'Another unhappy couple, apparently!' said someone at a table where three women were crocheting.

'They might wash their dirty linen elsewhere! Such a bad example for children!'

The two silhouettes met at the edge of the water. Not a word could be heard, but the attitudes made it easy to guess what was going on.

The man implored and threatened, the woman proved obdurate. Once he took hold of her wrist and it looked as if it were going to degenerate into a fight. But no, he turned his back on her. He walked with long strides towards a near-by road where he started up a little grey car.

'Waiter, another half-pint!'

Maigret had just noticed that the young woman had left her handbag on the table. It was imitation crocodile, full to bursting, quite new.

A shadow advanced along the ground.

He raised his head and saw the face of the owner of the bag as she reached the terrace.

He got a slight shock. His nostrils quivered.

Of course he might be mistaken. It was an impression rather than a certainty. But he could have sworn that before him stood the original of the portrait without a head.

Discreetly he took it out of his pocket. The woman had sat down again.

'Well, waiter! Where's my lemonade?'

'I thought . . . The gentleman said . . .'

'I ordered a lemonade!'

It was the rather fleshy line of the neck, the bosom, full but firm, voluptuously resilient.

The same way of dressing and the same taste in glossy silks in loud colours.

Maigret dropped the portrait so that his neighbour couldn't help seeing it.

And she did see it. She looked at the inspector as if she were trying to place him in her memory. But if she was worried she did not show it.

Five minutes, ten minutes passed. Then the purr of a car came from far off and grew louder. The grey car approached the terrace, stopped and started again as if the driver could not make up his mind definitely to go away.

'Gaston! . . .'

She stood up and made signs to her friend. This time she seized her bag, and a moment later she was in the car.

The three women at the next table followed her with disapproving eyes. The young man with the kodak turned round.

The grey car was already disappearing with its engine throbbing.

'Waiter. . . . Where can one get a car?'

'I don't think you'll find one in Yport. There is one that sometimes takes people to Fécamp or Etretat, but just today I saw it going off with some English people . . .'

The inspector's large fingers drummed a rapid tattoo on the table.

'Give me a road map. And get me the Fécamp police station on the telephone. . . . Have you ever seen those people before?'

'The ones who were quarrelling? Nearly every day this week. They lunched here yesterday. I think they come from Le Havre . . .'

All the families had gone from the beach, which was now bathed in the stillness of a summer evening. A black boat gravitated imperceptibly towards the line of the horizon, went into the sun and came out at the other side as if through a paper hoop.

4. Under the Sign of Mars

'I myself,' said the Fécamp Superintendent of Police, sharpening a blue pencil, 'must confess I haven't any illusions. It's very seldom that one clears up these sea affairs. Just suppose you try to find out the real truth about one of these common squabbles that break out every day in port. When my men arrive on the scene they're hard at it. But when they see the uniforms they all get together and turn on them. Question them; they all lie. They contradict each other. They complicate matters to such an extent that finally one just gives up . . .'

There were four of them smoking in the office, which was already filled with tobacco-smoke. It was evening. The superintendent of the Le Havre *Brigade Mobile*, who was officially in charge of the case, was accompanied by a young inspector.

Maigret was there in a private capacity. Seated in a corner beside a table, he had said nothing.

'But it seems quite simple to me!' ventured the young inspector, hoping to gain his chief's approval. 'Robbery wasn't the motive. Therefore it was a case of revenge. Who was Captain Fallut most severe with in the course of the trip?'

But the superintendent from Le Havre shrugged his shoulders and the inspector relapsed into silence, blushing.

'And yet . . .'

'No, my boy, no. There's something else. First of all, this woman you've unearthed, Maigret. You've given full particulars so that the police can find her again? For instance, I can't quite place her rôle.... The boat was away three months. She wasn't even there when they went off, since no one notified us.... The operator is engaged to be married.... Captain Fallut, from all accounts, doesn't seem the sort of man to do anything foolish.... And yet he drew up his will just before he was murdered.'

'It would also be interesting to know who took the trouble to bring the will here,' sighed Maigret. 'There's a little journalist, the one who always wears a beige mackintosh, who declares in the *Eclair de Rouen* that the *Océan* was sent by her owners on a mission quite other than cod-fishing...'

'They say that every time!' growled the Fécamp superintendent.

The conversation languished. There was a long silence in which the sucking of Maigret's pipe could be heard. Then he suddenly rose with an effort.

'If you were to ask me what was characteristic about this affair,' he said, 'I should say that it stands under the sign of Mars. Everybody belonging to that boat is quarrelsome, irritable, short-tempered. At the *Rendez-Vous des Terre-Neuvas* the crew gets drunk and fights. When I take the operator's fiancée to him, he can scarcely conceal his impatience and gives her a very chilly welcome. He practically told her to mind her own business! At Yport, the chief engineer gives his wife hell and treats me like a dog. Finally I find two other people who seem to come under the same influence: the woman called Adèle and her companion have a quarrel on the beach and only make it up so that they can get away.'

'What conclusions do you come to, then?' inquired the Le Havre superintendent.

'Me? No conclusions at all! I'm just remarking that I feel as if I were moving in a circle of maniacs.... Well,

good evening, gentlemen. Down here I am an amateur.
My wife is waiting for me at the hotel. You'll let me
know, Superintendent, if they find the Yport woman and
the man in the grey car?'

'Of course! Good night . . .'

Instead of going through the town, Maigret lounged
along the quays, his hands in his pockets, his pipe between his teeth. The empty dock made a vast black
rectangle reflecting the lights of the *Océan*, which was
still being unloaded.

'. . . Under the sign of Mars!' he growled to himself.

No one paid any attention to him when he went on
board. He walked apparently aimlessly along the bridge
and saw a light in the fo'c's'le deck hatchway. He
stooped down and was greeted by a warm breath of air,
the smell of a barrack-room, a refectory, and a fish shop,
all combined.

He went down the iron ladder and found himself face
to face with three men who were eating out of mess-tins
held between their knees. For light they had an oil-lamp
hung from a swivel. In the middle of the fo'c's'le was a
cast-iron stove encrusted with slag.

Along the bulkheads were four tiers of bunks, some
still filled with straw, others empty. Boots and sou'-
westers were hanging about.

The only one of the three who rose was P'tit Louis.
The other two were the Breton and a Negro with bare
feet.

'*Bon appetit!*' growled Maigret.

There were answering growls.

'Where are your pals?'

'In their homes, what do you think?' said P'tit Louis.
'It's only when you've nowhere to go to, and not a cent
in your pocket, that you stay here when the boat's in
dock.'

You had to get gradually accustomed to the semi-darkness, and especially to the smell. And you could imagine the same place when forty men lived there, unable to make a single movement without knocking into the others.

Forty men throwing themselves into their bunks with their boots on, snoring, chewing, smoking!

'Did the captain come here sometimes?'

'Never!'

And then the panting of machinery, the smell of coal and soot, the burning metal bulkheads, the battering blows of the sea . . .

'Come with me, P'tit Louis.'

And Maigret caught the sailor making signs behind his back to show off before the others.

But up above, on the shadowy bridge, all his swank had gone.

'What is it?'

'Nothing. . . . Listen. . . . Suppose the captain had died during the trip. Is there anyone who could have brought the ship into port?'

'Perhaps there isn't. . . . Because the second officer can't take the bearings. It's true they say that with the wireless the operator can always tell the position . . .'

'Did you see him often, the operator?'

'Never! You don't think we wander about then as we're doing now? Each man has his place. You stay in your corner for days on end . . .'

'And the chief engineer?'

'Oh, yes. We used to see *him* every day, so to speak.'

'What was he like?'

P'tit Louis became evasive.

'How should I know, after all? . . . And what is it you're trying to get at? You ought to be there when everything goes wrong – a cabin-boy overboard, a boiler feed-pipe burst, the captain insisting on taking the boat where there's not a single fish, a man with gangrene, et cetera. . . . You'd swear yourself black in the face. And for the least thing you'd let fly with your fist at anybody's mug! And when they say above that the captain up there is barmy . . .'

'Was he?'

'I didn't go and ask him. . . Then . . .'

'Then?'

'Well, after all, there can't be any harm. . . . There's sure to be someone who'll tell you. . . . It appears that the three of them, up there, were never without their revolvers. Three of them watching each other, frightened of each other. The captain hardly ever came out of his cabin, where he'd taken the map, the compass, the sextant, and all the rest . . .'

'And this went on for three months?'

'Yes! Have you anything else to ask me?'

'Thanks. . . . You can go . . .'

P'tit Louis seemed to be sorry to go, and stayed a moment by the hatchway watching the inspector puffing away at his pipe.

They were still bringing cod out of the yawning hold by the light of acetylene lamps. But the detective wanted to forget trucks, dock-labourers, quays, jetties, and lighthouses.

He was in a world of sheet-iron, and with half-closed eyes he pictured the open sea, the even ground-swell through which the bow of the ship ploughed its way without respite, hour after hour, day after day, week after week.

'You don't think we wander about then as we're doing now?'

Men at the engines. Men in the fore. And, aft in the poop, a handful of human beings: the captain, his second officer, the chief engineer, and the radio operator.

A little binnacle-lamp to light the compass. Maps spread out.

Three months!

When they got back, Captain Fallut had made a will in which he declared his intention of putting an end to his days.

An hour after the ship put into port, he was strangled and thrown into the dock.

And Madame Bernard, his landlady, was desolate because this made their admirably planned union for ever impossible! The chief engineer made scenes with his wife! A certain Adèle gave an unknown man hell, but made off with him the moment Maigret put her portrait scored with red ink under her nose!

The operator, Le Clinche, in his prison, was like a bear with a sore head!

The ship moved slightly, just a very light motion like the rise and fall of a bosom. One of the three men on the fo'c's'le deck was playing an accordion.

Maigret turned his head and saw on the quay two female silhouettes. He rushed forward and crossed the gangway.

'What are you doing here?'

He blushed because he had spoken harshly, more especially because he was conscious that he in his turn had been infected by this frenzy which had seized all the protagonists of the drama.

'We just wanted to see the ship,' said Madame Maigret with disarming humility.

'It's my fault!' Marie Léonnec interrupted. 'It was I who insisted.'

'All right! All right! Have you had dinner?'

'Why, yes! It's ten o'clock. Have you?'

'Yes. . . . Thank you . . .'

The *Rendez-Vous des Terre-Neuvas* was almost the only place still showing lights. On the jetty one could just make out some silhouettes: summer visitors conscientiously taking their evening stroll.

'You've discovered something?' asked Le Clinche's fiancée.

'Not yet. At least, not much.'

'I daren't ask you a favour . . .'

'Go on!'

'I should like to see Pierre's cabin. Will you allow me?'

He took her there with a shrug of his shoulders. Madame Maigret refused to cross the gangway.

It was a regular metal box. Wireless apparatus. A sheet-iron table, a bench, and a bunk. On the bulkhead a portrait of Marie Léonnec in Breton costume. Old shoes on the floor and a pair of trousers on the bunk.

The girl took in this atmosphere with a mixture of curiosity and pleasure.

'Yes! . . . It's not quite as I imagined. . . . His shoes haven't once been cleaned. Look! He always drank out of this glass without washing it . . .'

A funny girl! A mixture of timidity, weakness, good education, and on the other hand, energy and audacity. She hesitated.

'And the captain's cabin?'

Maigret gave a faint smile, for he realized that in her secret heart she hoped to make some discovery. He led her to it. He even went and got a lantern which he found on the bridge.

'How can they live in this smell? . . .' she sighed.

She looked attentively round her. He saw that she was rather timid and embarrassed as she asked:

'Why has the bed been raised up?'

He let his pipe go out. The observation was apt. All the crew slept in bunks which were somehow a part of the architectural scheme of the boat. Only the captain had an iron bedstead.

And under each foot a block of wood had been placed,

'Don't you find it strange? You'd think . . .'

'Go on.'

'You'd think – but you'll laugh at me! – that the bed had been raised so that someone could hide under it. Without the pieces of wood the mattress would be far too low . . . whereas like this . . .'

Every trace of ill-humour had vanished. He saw the girl's pale face strained with mental effort and excitement.

And before he could stop her she lay down on the floor, in spite of all the dirt, and slid under the bed.

'There *is* room!' she said.

'All right. . . . Come out . . .'

'One moment, please. Pass me the lamp a moment, Inspector!'

She was silent. He couldn't think what she was doing. He began to get impatient.

'Well?'

'Yes. . . . Wait . . .'

She got up suddenly, her grey suit all dirty, her eyes fevered.

'Pull out the bed. . . . You'll see . . .'

Her voice was broken. Her hands trembled. Maigret pulled the bed savagely away from the bulkhead and looked on the ground.

'I don't see anythnig.'

As she made no answer, he turned round and found that she was crying.

'What did you see? . . . What are you crying for? . . .'

'Here. . . . Read . . .'

He had to get right down and hold the lamp up against the bulkhead. Then he made out some words written on the wood with some pointed object, a pin or a nail.

'*Gaston . . . Octave . . . Pierre . . . Hen . . .*'

The last word was unfinished. Yet it had not been done

in a hurry. Some of the letters must have taken over an hour! There were the sort of strokes and flourishes one makes when one has nothing better to do.

The comic note was struck by two stags' antlers which had been drawn over the name 'Octave'.

The girl sat on the edge of the bed, which had been dragged into the middle of the cabin. She was still weeping silently.

'Curious!' growled Maigret. 'I should very much like to know whether . . .'

She rose vehemently.

'Of course! That's what it was! There was a woman here! She hid. But it didn't keep men from finding her. . . . Wasn't Captain Fallut's name Octave?'

The inspector had rarely been so embarrassed.

'Don't draw hasty conclusions!' he said, without the slightest conviction.

'But it's written! The whole story's there! Four men who . . .'

What could he say to calm her?

'Take it from my experience. In police matters you must always wait before you jump to conclusions. You told me just yesterday that Le Clinche is incapable of killing anyone . . .'

'Yes!' she sobbed. 'Yes! I believe it! That's true!'

She clung to this hope in spite of everything.

'But his name's Pierre!'

'I know. . . . Well? Every tenth sailor is called Pierre, and there were fifty men on board. . . . There is also the matter of a Gaston and a Henry . . .'

'What do you think?'

'Nothing!'

'Are you going to show this to the magistrate? . . . When I think that it was I who . . .'

'Keep calm! We have discovered nothing at all yet, except that the bed has been raised for some reason or another, and that someone has written those Christian names on the bulkhead . . .'

'There was a woman . . .'

'Why a woman?'

'But . . .'

'Come along! Madame Maigret is waiting for us on the quay . . .'

'That's true . . .'

She wiped her tears obediently between sniffs.

'I shouldn't have come. . . . And I thought . . . But it's not possible that Pierre . . . Listen! I must see him as soon as possible. I'll talk to him, quite alone. . . . You'll do what's necessary, won't you?'

Before she set foot on the gangway she cast a look charged with hatred on the black ship which was no longer the same to her now that she knew that a woman had hidden on board.

Madame Maigret looked curiously at her.

'Come now, don't cry! You know it will all turn out all right . . .'

'No! No!' She shook her head in despair.

She could not speak. She was choking. She wanted to look back at the ship. And Madame Maigret, who didn't understand at all, looked inquiringly at her husband.

'Take her back to the hotel. Try to calm her . . .'

'Has anything happened? . . .'

'Nothing definite. . . . I'll probably be a bit late . . .'

He watched them as they went off. Marie Léonnec turned back a dozen times, and her companion had to drag her along like a child.

Maigret almost went back on board. But he was thirsty. There was still a light at the *Rendez-Vous des Terre-Neuvas*.

At one table four sailors were playing cards. Near the bar, a young admirer had passed an arm round the barmaid's waist, and from time to time she gave a little laugh.

The proprietor was following the game and giving advice.

'Hello! It's you ...' was his greeting to Maigret.

And he didn't seem particularly happy to see him again. On the contrary, he couldn't hide a slight embarrassment.

'Go on, Julie. ... Serve the inspector. ... What can I offer you?'

'Nothing at all. If you'll allow me, I'll order a drink like anyone else ...'

'No offence! ... I ...'

Was the day going to end under the sign of Mars? One of the sailors growled something in Norman patois, and Maigret managed to translate roughly:

'Well, well! Still snooping round ...'

The inspector looked him in the eyes. He blushed and stammered:

'I'll bid a club!'

'You should have bid spades!' said Léon, for something to say.

5. Adèle and Her Companion

The telephone bell rang. Léon ran to answer it, and immediately called Maigret.

'Hello!' said a bored voice at the other end of the wire. 'Inspector Maigret? This is the clerk at the Police Station. I've just rung your hotel and they said I would perhaps find you at the *Rendez-Vous des Terre-Neuvas*. ... Sorry to bother you, Inspector. I've been on the line half an hour ... I can't get the chief. ... As for the superintendent of the *Brigade Mobile*, I'm wondering whether

49

he's left Fécamp. . . . Well, I've got two queer cards here who have just come in, and it seems they've got some important statement to make . . . a man and a woman . . .'

'With a grey car?'

'Yes. Are those the ones you were looking for?'

Ten minutes later, Maigret arrived at the police station. The offices were deserted, except for the inquiry office, which was divided in two by a rail.

The clerk was writing and smoking a cigarette. Seated on a bench, his elbows on his knees, his chin between his hands, a man was waiting.

And finally there was a woman walking up and down, stamping on the floor with her high heels.

When the inspector came in she marched up to him, and at the same time the man rose with a sigh of relief, muttering between his teeth:

'Well, you've kept us long enough!'

It was the Yport couple, even more ill-tempered than during the scene Maigret had witnessed.

'Will you follow me? . . .'

And he took them into the superintendent's office, sat down on his swivel-chair and lit a pipe, watching them all the time.

'You can sit down.'

'Thank you!' said the woman, who was decidedly the more nervous of the two. 'We've been doing nothing else for a long time.'

He now saw her face to face by the strong light of an electric lamp. It didn't need a long examination to place her. The portrait, with only the bust left, had been quite enough.

A fine figure of a woman, in the popular acceptance of the word. A woman with an attractive body, sound teeth, a provocative smile, and an eye that was always animated.

In other words, a fine bitch, flighty, greedy, equally

ready to make a scene or to burst into a great vulgar laugh.

Her blouse was pink silk, caught with a gold brooch the size of a hundred-centime piece.

'First, I insist on telling you . . .'

'Excuse me!' interrupted Maigret. 'Will you sit down as I asked you and answer my questions.'

She frowned. Her mouth took on an ugly expression.

'Listen! You forget I'm here of my own free will . . .'

Her companion made a face, bored with this attitude. They were well matched. He was just the sort of man usually found with that sort of woman.

He hadn't exactly a hang-dog look. He was dressed correctly, but in bad taste. He had big rings on his fingers and a pearl in his tie. But his ensemble wasn't right.

He was the sort of man seen in cafés and restaurants at all hours drinking champagne with women, and putting up at third-rate hotels.

'You first! Your name, domicile, and profession . . .'

He attempted to get up.

'Stay where you are!'

'I'm going to explain . . .'

'Nothing of the sort! Your name . . .'

'Gaston Buzier. At the moment my business is selling and letting villas. I mostly live at Le Havre at the *Anneau d'Argent* hotel . . .'

'Are you an established estate agent?'

'No . . . but . . .'

'Are you employed in any agency?'

'Well . . .'

'That's enough. In a word, you're a shyster. How were you employed previously?'

'I was representative of a make of bicycles. . . . I've also gone round getting orders for sewing-machines . . .'

'How many convictions?'

'Don't answer, Gaston!' interrupted the woman. 'This is a hell of a note! It's we who came to . . .'

'Shut up! Two convictions. One, with delay of execution, on account of a rubber check. . . . Another for two months for not having given the owner the full amount I'd received on a villa. . . . You see, they're mere nothings . . .'

One felt that he, anyway, was used to facing the police. He remained at his ease, with a touch of malice in his expression.

'Your turn!' said Maigret, turning to the woman.

'Adèle Noirhomme . . . born at Belleville . . .'

'Registered?'

'They put me on the register at Strasbourg five years ago, because a woman had it in for me for vamping her husband. But since then . . .'

'You've managed to escape police control. . . . Fine! Will you tell me in what capacity you sailed on the *Océan*?'

'I must first explain!' answered the man. 'The fact that we've come here shows that we've nothing to reproach ourselves for. At Yport Adèle came and told me you'd got her photograph and were sure to arrest us. . . . Our first idea was to get out to avoid any trouble . . . because we know the police racket. . . . At Etretat I saw gendarmes on the lookout and I knew we were going to be nabbed. So I preferred to come here of my own accord . . .'

'Your turn, madame! I asked you what you were doing on the trawler . . .'

'That's quite simple – I was following my lover!'

'Captain Fallut?'

'Yes, the captain! I've been with him, so to speak, since November. We met at a café in Le Havre. . . . He fell in love. . . . He came back two or three times a week. Right from the beginning I thought he was mad because he never asked for anything – but he was just struck on me. He took a nicely furnished room for me, and I thought that, if I set about it in the right way, he'd end up by marrying me. Sailors aren't rolling in money, but they're regular and there's always the pension . . .'

'You never came to Fécamp with him?'

'No! He forbade me. It was he who came over here. He was jealous. The sort of chap that can't have had much experience, because at fifty he was as timid with women as a schoolboy. . . . And yet, when he was mad about me . . .'

'Excuse me! You were already the mistress of Gaston Buzier?'

'Of course. But I introduced Gaston to Fallut as my brother.'

'I understand. In short, both of you were living on the captain's money.'

'I was working . . .' Buzier protested.

'I know! Every Saturday afternoon! – Who thought of taking you on board?'

'Fallut! The idea of leaving me alone during the entire trip was worrying him. . . . On the other hand, he was scared stiff, because the regulations are strict and he was a stickler for regulations. . . . Up to the last moment he hesitated. Then he came to get me. He made me go into his cabin the night before they sailed. The idea of a change amused me, but if I'd known how it was going to turn out I'd have dropped it like a hot coal!'

'Didn't Buzier protest?'

'He was a bit doubtful. But, you know, he didn't want to go against the old boy's ideas. He'd promised to retire straight away after the trip and marry me. A fine life he had in store for me! Shut up all day in a cabin stinking of fish! And what's more, when anyone came in I had to hide under the bed! . . . We'd hardly put out to sea when Fallut regretted having taken me. . . . I've never seen a man with such moods as he had. Ten times a day he'd come to see whether the door was properly locked. If I spoke, he made me shut up for fear anyone should hear me. He was sulky and irritable. He even used to give me dirty looks as if he were tempted to get rid of me by throwing me overboard . . .'

Her voice became shrill and she waved her arms about.

'Not to mention the fact that he got more and more jealous! He questioned me about my past. He tried to find out. For three days he didn't speak to me, just watched me like an enemy. Then suddenly his passion would get hold of him again. There were times when I was afraid of him . . .'

'Which of the members of the crew saw you on board?'

'It was on the fourth night. I wanted to go on the bridge for a breath of air . . . I'd had enough of being shut up. Fallut went to make sure there was no one about. He only just allowed me to take about five steps up and down. He had to go down to the deck for a moment, and it was then the operator came and talked to me. He was very shy, but in a fever. . . . The next day he managed to get into my cabin . . .'

'Did Fallut see him?'

'I don't think so – he didn't say anything . . .'

'You became Le Clinche's mistress?'

She made no answer. Gaston Buzier sneered.

'Go on, tell him!' he snapped at her in a nasty voice.

'I'm free to do what I like! It's not as if you had kept off women while I was away. Eh? What about the little thing at the *Villa des Fleurs*? And that photo I found in your pocket . . .'

Maigret remained impassive as a graven image.

'I asked you whether you became the radio operator's mistress . . .'

'And I say go to blazes!'

She was being provocative, with her moist smile. She

54

knew she was desirable. She was reckoning on her full lips, her inviting body.

'The chief engineer saw you too?'

'What has he been telling you?'

'Nothing! I will sum up. The captain kept you hidden in his cabin. In turn Pierre Le Clinche and the chief engineer came secretly to see you.... Did Fallut find out?'

'No!'

'All the same, he must have had his suspicions, for he kept prowling round you, only leaving you when it was strictly necessary...'

'How do you know?'

'Did he still talk of marrying you?'

'I don't know...'

And Maigret saw the ship, the stokers isolated in their hold, the men packed together in the fo'c's'le, the operator's cabin and the captain's aft, with the raised bed.

And the trip had lasted three months!

And all this time three men had been prowling round the cabin where the woman was shut up.

'A damn silly thing I did!' she exclaimed. 'I swear that if I could begin all over again.... One should always mistrust those timid men who talk of marriage...'

'If you'd listened to me...' interrupted Gaston Buzier.

'You shut up! If I'd listened to you, I know what kind of house I'd be in at this time of day! ... I don't want to speak ill of Fallut now that he's dead. But he was touchy, all the same. He got ideas about things ... he would have thought himself dishonoured just because he'd broken the regulations. And it went from bad to worse.... After a week he never opened his mouth except to make scenes – or else to ask whether anyone had been into the cabin! He was particularly jealous of

Le Clinche and he used to say: "That would please you, eh! A young man! ... Confess that if he came in while I was away you wouldn't repulse him!"

'And he'd sneer until you felt quite ill ...'

'How many times was Le Clinche together with you?' Maigret asked slowly.

'Oh, well, who cares anyway! ... Once. On the fourth day. I couldn't even tell you how it happened. ... Afterwards it wasn't possible because Fallut watched me too closely ...'

'And the engineer?'

'Never! He tried. ... He'd come and look through the porthole. ... Always with a dead pale face. ... You can't imagine what a life that was – I was like a beast in a cage. When there was a bit of a swell I used to be sick and Fallut didn't even bother to attend to me. For weeks he wouldn't touch me, then it would get hold of him. He would kiss me as if he wanted to bite me, and embrace me as if he'd like to stifle me ...'

Gaston Buzier had lit a cigarette and was smoking away with an ironical expression.

'You'll notice, Inspector, that I don't come into it. ... All this time I was working ...'

'Will you please stop it?' she said impatiently.

'What happened when you got back? Had Fallut announced his intention of killing himself?'

'He? Certainly not! ... When we got into port he hadn't spoken a word to me for a fortnight. What's more, I don't believe he'd spoken to anyone. He spent hours staring straight in front of him. I'd decided to leave him anyway ... I was fed up, you see. I'd rather starve and have my freedom. ... I heard that we were coming into port. He came into the cabin and just said these few words: "You'll wait until I come and fetch you ..."'

'Go on!'

'That's all I know. Or rather, Gaston told me the rest. . . . He was on the quay!'

'You tell me,' Maigret said to him.

'I was on the quay, as she says. I saw the sailors going into the café. I was waiting for Adèle. It was very dark. . . . Then the captain came off, quite alone. . . . There were some stationary trucks. . . . He took a few steps and then a man fell on him. . . . I don't know exactly what happened, but there was the noise of a body falling into the water . . .'

'Would you recognize the man?'

'No! It was very dark and the trucks hid nearly everything.'

'What direction did he take?'

'I think he went along the quay . . .'

'And you didn't see the operator?'

'I don't know . . . I've never seen him . . .'

Maigret turned to the woman.

'Now you, how did you get out of the cabin?'

'Someone opened the cabin door where I was locked up. It was Le Clinche. He said to me: "Get out quick!"'

'Is that all?'

'I wanted to question him. I heard people running on the quay, and saw a boat coming up the dock with a lamp. . . . But he said again: "Get out." He pushed me on to the gangway. Everyone was looking in another direction. They didn't notice me. . . . I was pretty sure something dirty was going on, but I preferred to get away. . . . Gaston was waiting a little farther along . . .'

'And what did you do after that?'

'Gaston was quite pale. We went and had some rum in a pub. We slept at the Railway Hotel. . . . The next day all the papers were talking about Fallut's death. . . . Then we started and got away to Le Havre, just as a precaution. We didn't want to get mixed up in that business . . .'

'But that didn't prevent her from wanting to hang round here,' snapped her lover. 'I don't know whether it was for the operator or . . .'

'You shut up! . . . That's quite enough. . . . Naturally I was interested in the business. As a matter of fact, we came three times to Fécamp. And so as not to be noticed, we slept at Yport . . .'

'You didn't see the chief engineer again?'

'How do you know? One day at Yport. . . . Though the look he gave me made me quite frightened. He followed me for some time . . .'

'Why were you quarrelling with your lover just now?'

She shrugged her shoulders.

'Because! Haven't you understood yet? He's convinced I'm in love with Le Clinche, that it's for me the operator did the murder, et cetera. . . . He's been making scenes and I'm fed up! I saw enough on the cursed boat . . .'

'All the same, when I showed you your photo on the terrace . . .'

'That was a dirty trick! Of course I realized you were from the police! I thought Le Clinche must have talked. I got the wind up and I told Gaston to get us out of it. . . . It was only when we'd gone that it occurred to us it was no good, that you'd get us in the end. Not to mention the fact that we'd only two hundred francs in our pockets. . . . What are you going to do with me? You can't put me in prison?'

'You think it's the operator who did the murder?'

'How should I know?'

'Do you possess a pair of yellow shoes?' Maigret asked Gaston Buzier brutally.

'I. . . Yes. . . Why?'

'Nothing. I was just asking. Are you sure you wouldn't be able to recognize the murderer of the captain?'

'I only saw a silhouette in the dark . . .'

'Well! Pierre Le Clinche was there too, hiding among the trucks, and he says that the murderer was wearing yellow shoes.'

Buzier sprang up, his eyes hard, a sneer on his lips.

'He said that? You're sure he said that?'

He choked and stuttered with rage. He was quite transformed. He looked challengingly round the room.

'Take me to him. I insist! By God, I insist! And then we'll see who's lying! Yellow shoes! So it's me, eh? He takes my woman. . . . He takes her off the boat. . . . And he has the gall to say . . .'

'Quietly . . .'

He couldn't get breath.

'You hear that, Adèle?' he panted. 'That's what they're like, your lovers!'

Tears of rage gushed from his eyes. His teeth chattered.

'My God! So it was me! Ha! ha! That's rich! That's better than the movies! And of course, as I'd two convictions, you knew I'd done it! I killed Captain Fallut. Because I was jealous of him, perhaps? And then what? Haven't I killed the operator as well?'

He passed a hand through his hair with a feverish gesture, rumpling it up. It made him look thinner, deepened the shadows under his eyes and made his skin look duller.

'What are you waiting for? Why don't you arrest me?'

'Shut up!' muttered Adèle.

But she was getting a bit desperate too, although it didn't prevent her from shooting keen glances at her companion.

Did she have her doubts? Or was she only bluffing?

'If you must arrest me, do it at once! But I demand that you let me meet the gentleman face to face. . . .Then we'll see!'

Maigret pressed an electric bell, and the superintendent's secretary put in a worried face.

'You'll lock up this lady and gentleman until the magistrate decides what is to be done.'

'Swine!' cried Adèle, and spat on the floor. 'Catch me telling the truth again. And first of all, everything that I said I just made up – so there. And I won't sign any statement. Carry on with your scheme.... So that's what it was!'

Then, turning to her lover, she went on:

'Don't worry, Gaston! It'll be all right. And you'll see that in the end we'll come out on top! Only, of course, once a woman's had her name put on the register, she's only fit for locking up.... But wasn't it me, perhaps, who killed the captain? ...'

Maigret went out without listening to any more. Outside he breathed down gulps of sea air and knocked the ashes out of his pipe. Before he'd gone ten steps he heard Adèle's voice in the police station hurling all the foulest words in her vocabulary at the policemen.

It was two in the morning. The night was calm and unreal. The tide was high and the masts of the fishing-boats swayed above the roofs of the houses.

Over all was a rhythmic murmur, wave after wave breaking on the shore.

There were glaring lights round the *Océan*. Day and night the unloading went on and porters pushed the full trucks, bending their backs under the weight.

The *Rendez-Vous des Terre Neuvas* was closed. At the *Hôtel de la Plage* the porter, a pair of trousers over his night-shirt, opened the door to the inspector.

A single light was burning in the hall. That was why Maigret did not at first see the figure of a woman in a cane-chair.

It was Marie Léonnec. She was asleep with her head on her shoulder.

'I think she's waiting for you . . .' whispered the porter.

She was pale, one might almost say anaemic. Her lips were colourless and dark circles round her eyes betrayed her fatigue. She slept with her mouth a little open, as if she couldn't get enough air.

Maigret touched her gently on the shoulder. She jumped up, pulled herself together and looked at him confusedly.

'I was asleep . . . oh!'

'Why didn't you go to bed? Didn't my wife take you to your room?'

'Yes, but I crept down again. I wanted to know! Tell me . . .'

She wasn't as pretty as usual . . . sleep had made her skin damp. And a mosquito bite had left a red spot in the middle of her forehead.

Her dress, which she must have made herself out of some durable serge, was crumpled.

'Have you discovered anything new? No? . . . Listen! I've been doing a lot of thinking. I don't know how to say it to you. Before I see Pierre tomorrow, I'd like you to talk to him, to tell him I know all about this woman and that I'm not angry with him. I'm sure, you see, that he's not guilty. Only, if I speak to him first, he'll be embarrassed. You saw him this morning . . . he's letting it prey on his mind. After all, it's quite natural, if there was a woman on board, for him to . . .'

But it was beyond her! She broke out into sobs. She couldn't stop crying.

'Above all, this mustn't get into the papers in case my parents get to know. They wouldn't understand . . . they . . .'

She gulped.

'You *must* find the murderer! It seems to me that if *I* could only question people . . . Excuse me! I don't know what I'm saying. You know better than I do. Only you don't know Pierre. I'm two years older than him. He's like a child. And, if he's accused, he's capable of shutting up, from sheer pride, and saying nothing. He is very sensitive. He's often been humiliated . . .'

Slowly Maigret put his hand on her shoulder and stifled a deep sigh.

Adèle's voice was still buzzing in his ears. He thought of her, provocatively animal, magnificently sensual.

And this girl, nicely brought up, anaemic, tried to stifle her sobs, to smile confidently.

'When you know him . . .'

But what *she* would never know was that black cabin round which three men had prowled, for days, for weeks, there in the middle of the sea, while the men at the engines, the men in the fo'c's'le, dimly sensed drama, watched the sea, discussed bearings, became uneasy and talked of madness and the evil eye.

'I'll see Le Clinche tomorrow . . .'

'But shall I?'

'Perhaps. Probably. You must go and lie down!'

And a little later, Madame Maigret, half-asleep, murmured:

'She's very nice. Do you know, she has all her trousseau ready? All hand-embroidered. Have you any news? You smell of scent . . .'

A little of Adèle's strong perfume must have clung to him. A perfume as common as the blue wine you get at a *bistro*. For months it had mingled on the trawler with the rank smell of cod, whilst three men prowled round and round a cabin, obstinate and surly as dogs.

'Sleep well!' he said as he drew the cover up to her chin.

And he imprinted a deep solemn kiss on his sleeping wife's forehead.

6. Three Who Were Innocent

The scene was simple, the usual setting for such meetings, in this case the little prison office. Superintendent Girard of Le Havre, who was in charge of the case, occupied the only chair. Maigret leaned against the black marble mantelpiece. On the walls were diagrams, official announcements, and a portrait of the President of the Republic.

Standing in the glare of the light was Gaston Buzier with his yellow shoes on.

'Bring in the radio operator!'

The door opened. Pierre Le Clinche, who had been told nothing, came forward frowning like a man who is suffering and awaits fresh trials. He saw Buzier, but he did not take any notice of him. He looked round, wondering where he should turn to.

Adèle's lover, however, scrutinized him from head to foot, his lip curling.

Le Clinche looked rumpled, and his face was grey. He neither tried to carry off nor to conceal his dejection. He was as miserable as a sick beast.

'Do you recognize the man in front of you?'

He looked at Buzier and seemed to search his memory.

'No! Who is he?'

'Look him over carefully.'

Le Clinche obeyed, and as soon as he came to his feet he raised his head.

'Well?'

'Yes . . .'

'What do you mean by "yes"?'

'I see what you mean. . . . The yellow shoes . . .'

'Exactly!' exploded Gaston Buzier, who had hitherto stood silent with a cantankerous expression on his face.

'Repeat that it was me who bumped off your captain. Well?'

All eyes were fixed on the operator, whose head drooped while he made a weary gesture with his hand.

'Speak.'

'Perhaps it wasn't those shoes . . .'

'Ha! ha!' Buzier was already exultant. 'So you're climbing down?'

'You don't identify Fallut's murderer?'

'I don't know. . . . No . . .'

'You are aware that you are in the presence of the lover of a certain Adèle whom you know. He has himself confessed that he was in the neighbourhood of the trawler at the time of the crime. And he was wearing yellow shoes.'

All this time Buzier was challenging him with a look, trembling with rage and impatience.

'Yes, let him talk! But let him try to tell the truth, or I swear . . .'

'You be quiet! Well, Le Clinche?'

He passed his hand across his forehead, and literally grimaced with pain.

'I don't know! He can go and hang himself!'

'Did you see a man with yellow shoes attack Fallut?'

'I've forgotten . . .'

'That's what you asserted the first time you were interrogated. And that's not so long ago. Do you stick to this statement?'

'Well, no, I don't! I saw a man with yellow shoes – that's all. I don't know whether he was the murderer. . . .'

As the interrogation proceeded, Gaston Buzier, also slightly the worse for wear after a night at the police station, recovered his self-assurance. He rocked from one foot to another, one hand in his trouser-pocket.

'You see, he's piping down! He doesn't dare repeat the lies he told you . . .'

'Answer me, Le Clinche. Up to now, we are certain that there were two people present near the trawler at the time of the murder. You on the one hand, Buzier on the other. . . . You say you didn't kill him. After accusing Buzier you seem to be withdrawing your accusation. Then might there have been a third person? In that case, you couldn't have failed to see him! . . . Who was it?'

Silence. Pierre Le Clinche stared at the ground.

Maigret, still leaning on the mantelpiece, had taken no part in the interrogation, letting his colleague speak and confining himself to observing the two men.

'I will repeat my question: Was there a third person on the quay?'

'I don't know . . .' sighed the accused brokenly.

'That means yes?'

A shrug of the shoulders signifying:

'If you like.'

'Who?'

'It was dark . . .'

'Well, tell me why you asserted that the murderer was wearing yellow shoes. Wasn't it to avert suspicion from the real murderer, whom you know?'

The young man pressed his forehead between his two hands.

'I can't go on . . .' he sobbed.

'Answer!'

'No! . . . Do what you like . . .'

'Bring in the next witness.'

The door opened again, and Adèle came forward with an exaggerated self-assurance. She gave a quick glance round the assembly, to try and make out what had been happening. She gave a specially long look at the operator, and seemed amazed to see him so overcome.

'Now, Le Clinche, I expect you recognize the woman

whom Captain Fallut kept concealed in his cabin throughout the entire journey, and whose lover you were. . .' He looked coldly at her, although Adèle's lips were already half-opened in an encouraging smile.

'That's her.'

'Briefly, there were three of you on the ship hanging round her: the captain, the chief engineer, and you. You possessed her at least once. . . . The chief engineer didn't succeed. . . . Did the captain know you had deceived him?'

'He never mentioned it to me.'

'He was very jealous, wasn't he? It was because of this jealousy that for three months he didn't say a single word to you?'

'No . . .'

'What? There was another reason?'

Le Clinche grew red and didn't know where to look; too quickly he stammered:

'That's to say, perhaps it was because of that – I don't know . . .'

'What other cause for hatred or mistrust was there between you?'

'I . . . There was none. . . . You were right. . . . He was jealous . . .'

'And what sentiment were you guided by on becoming Adèle's lover?'

Silence.

'You love her?'

'No!' he said curtly.

'Thank you!' shrilled the woman. 'You are polite, I must say! But that didn't prevent you from running round me up to the last day. Isn't that true? It's also true that there was probably someone else waiting for you on shore . . .'

Gaston Buzier affected to whistle, his fingers stuck in the armholes of his waistcoat.

'Tell me again, Le Clinche, whether, when you went back on board after witnessing the death of the captain, Adèle was really locked up in his cabin.'

'Locked up, yes . . .'

'So she couldn't have killed him? . . .'

'No, that wasn't it, I swear . . .'

Le Clinche was quite unnerved. But Superintendent Girard went on ponderously:

'Buzier states that you didn't do the murder. You, after accusing him, took it back. Another hypothesis is that the two of you were accomplices . . .'

'Thank you!' Buzier exploded with terrific scorn. 'When I get mixed up in a crime it won't be in the company of a . . . a . . .'

'That's enough! Both of you might have done the murder out of jealousy, as you both had Adèle as your mistress.'

Buzier sneered.

'Me jealous? . . . Of what?'

'Have you any further statement to make? You, Le Clinche?'

'No.'

'Buzier?'

'I insist that I am innocent and I demand to be set free.'

'And you?'

Adèle was making up her lips.

'Me?' – a dab of lipstick – 'I' – a look in her mirror – 'have nothing at all to say. All men are mugs! You heard this boy here, for whom I could maybe have done something pretty silly? You needn't look at me like that, Gaston. . . . Now, if you want my opinion, it is that in all this affair on the boat there are things we know nothing about. Just because there was a woman on board you thought that explained everything. But suppose it was something else?'

'Such as . . .?'

'I don't know . . . I'm not the police . . .'

She arranged her hair under her red straw toque. Maigret noticed that Le Clinche turned away his head.

The two detectives exchanged a look. Girard announced:

'Le Clinche will go back to his cell. You two will wait in the parlour. In a quarter of an hour I shall let you know whether you are free or not . . .'

The detectives were left alone, both rather worried.

'Are you going to propose to the examining magistrate that he should let them go?' asked Maigret.

'Yes! I think it's the best thing to do. They may be mixed up in the affair. At the same time, there are other elements that have escaped us . . .'

'*Parbleu*!'

'Hello! Give me the Le Havre Law Courts. . . . Hello! Yes, the Court!'

A little later, while Superintendent Girard was talking to the magistrate, there was a disturbance in the corridor. Maigret rushed out and saw Le Clinche lying on the ground struggling with three men in uniform.

He was in a terrible state of over-excitement. His bloodshot eyes were staring out of his head, his mouth dribbled. But, held down on every side, he could not move.

'What happened?'

'We hadn't bothered to put handcuffs on him as he'd always been so quiet. Then, coming down the corridor, he tried to take my revolver out of my belt. He got hold of it. . . . I managed to prevent him from pulling the trigger . . .'

Le Clinche lay on the ground, staring fixedly above him; his teeth bit into his lips, mixing blood with saliva.

The most disturbing thing about him was that tears were rolling down his wan cheeks.

'Should I get a doctor?'

'No! Leave him!' Maigret commanded.

And when they had gone, leaving him lying alone on the stone floor, he said:

'Get up! Come on! Quicker than that . . . and quietly! Or else you'll feel my fist in your face, silly fool that you are!'

The operator obeyed, docile and timid. His whole body was throbbing with fever and he had got dirty when he fell down.

'Where does your fiancée come in, in all this?'

Superintendent Girard came up.

'It's all right,' he said. 'They're free, all three of them, but they are not allowed to leave Fécamp. . . . What's been happening?'

'This fool tried to kill himself! If you'll allow me, I'll see to him . . .'

                              *

Together they walked along the quay. Le Clinche had dashed some cold water on his face, which still had red patches on it. His eyes were feverish, his lips too highly coloured.

He was wearing a ready-made three-buttoned grey suit, fastened without any regard for elegance. His tie was askew.

Maigret, his hands in his pockets, walked doggedly along, growling, seemingly to himself:

'You must understand that I've no time to lecture you. But there's one thing. Your fiancée is here. She's a brave little thing, who hurried here from Quimper and has been moving heaven and earth. It's no use driving her to despair . . .'

'She knows?'

'You don't need to tell her about that woman.'

Maigret watched him closely. They came to the end of the quays, the bright colours of the fishing-boats

69

blazed in the sun, the pavements were crowded.

Sometimes Le Clinche seemed to be taking an interest in life again: he would look round him hopefully, and then his eyes grew hard and he looked scornfully at people and things.

They had to pass quite near the *Océan*, where they were just finishing the unloading. There were three trucks left in front of the ship. Quite casually, Maigret murmured, indicating certain points: 'You were there . . . Gaston Buzier here. . . . And it was here that a third man strangled the captain . . .'

His companion took a deep breath and looked away.

'Only it was dark and you couldn't distinguish anyone. In any case, the third man was neither the chief engineer nor the second officer, because they were both with the crew in the *Rendez-Vous des Terre-Neuvas* . . .'

The Breton, who was on the bridge, saw the operator and went and leant over the hatchway. Three sailors emerged and looked at Le Clinche.

'Come!' said Maigret. 'Marie Léonnec is waiting for us.'

'I can't . . .'

'What can't you?'

'Go there. . . . Leave me, please! What difference can it make to you if I do away with myself? Particularly if it's going to be better for everyone!'

'Is the secret so burdensome, Le Clinche?'

Le Clinche was silent.

'And you can't possibly tell me anything, can you? . . . Yes! One thing! Do you still want Adèle?'

'I detest her!'

'I didn't say that! I said want, want her as you wanted her the whole of the trip. . . . We're men, Le Clinche. . . . Did you have many adventures before you knew Marie Léonnec?'

'No. . . . Nothing of importance . . .'

'And never that passion, that desire for a woman, that makes you fairly weep?'

'Never ...' He turned away his head.

'Then it was on board that it happened. There was only one woman in that bleak monotonous setting. Perfumed flesh in that trawler that stank of fish.... What did you say?'

'Nothing ...'

'You forgot about your fiancée?'

'It's not the same thing ...'

Maigret looked him in the face and was amazed at the change that had just taken place. His companion's brow had suddenly become purposeful, his look fixed, his lips bitter. And yet, in spite of it all, the nostalgia, the dreamy expression remained.

'Marie Léonnec is pretty ...' Maigret went on, following up his idea.

'Yes ...'

'And much more distinguished than Adèle. What's more, she loves you. She's ready to make any sacrifice to ...'

'Oh, do stop it!' groaned the operator. 'You know perfectly well that – that ...'

'That it's different! Marie Léonnec is a nice girl, will make a model wife and a good mother, but ... There'll always be something lacking, won't there? Something more violent. Something that you knew on board, hidden in the captain's cabin, fear constricting your throat a little, in Adèle's arms. Something vulgar and brutal. ... Adventure ... and the desire to bite, to do something desperate, to kill or to die ...'

Le Clinche listened in amazement.

'How do you ...?'

'How do I know? Because everyone experiences that sense of adventure at least once in his life.... You weep! You cry out! You die! Then, a fortnight after, when you see Marie Léonnec, you wonder how you can have been excited by an Adèle . . .'

While he was walking along, the young man gazed at the mirroring waters of the harbour, the distorted reflections of the boat-hulls, red, white, or green.

'The trip's over. . . . Adèle's gone. . . . Marie Léonnec is here . . .'

There was a moment of calm.

'The crisis was dramatic,' Maigret went on. 'A man died because there was passion on board and . . .'

But Le Clinche's fever flared up again :

'Stop it! Stop it!' he repeated in a dry voice. 'No! You see perfectly well that it's not possible . . .'

His eyes were haggard. He turned back to look at the trawler which, nearly empty now, stood monstrous and high in the water.

He was again seized with terror.

'I swear . . . You must let me go . . .'

'The captain was in distress too during the whole trip, wasn't he?'

'What do you mean?'

'And the chief engineer?'

'No . . .'

'There were only you two, then. It was fear, wasn't it, Le Clinche?'

'I don't know. . . . Leave me alone, for heaven's sake!'

'Adèle was in the cabin. There were three men hanging round. And yet the captain wouldn't yield to his desire, spent days and days without speaking to his mistress. And you watched her through the port-hole, but after a single meeting you never touched her again . . .'

'Stop it!'

'The men in the hold, the men on duty, spoke of the evil eye, and the trip went from bad to worse – bad seamanship, an accident, the cabin-boy overboard, two men

72

injured, the cod gone wrong, and the entrance into port bungled . . .'

They turned a corner of the quay, and the beach lay before them, with its neat esplanade, its hotels, its bathing-huts, and the multi-coloured deck-chairs on the sand.

In a pool of sunlight was Madame Maigret, sitting on a deck-chair beside Marie Léonnec in a white hat.

Le Clinche followed his companion's glance and stopped dead, his forehead damp.

'One woman wouldn't cause all that. Come on! Your fiancée has seen you . . .'

It was true. She rose. For a moment she remained motionless, as if her feelings were too strong for her. Then she rushed along the esplanade, while Madame Maigret put down her sewing and waited.

7. In the Family Circle

It was one of those situations which spring up of themselves and which it is very difficult to get out of. Marie Léonnec, alone in Fécamp and recommended to the Maigrets by a mutual friend, took her meals with them.

Now her fiancé was there. The four of them found themselves together on the beach when the hotel gong sounded for lunch.

There was some hesitation on Pierre Le Clinche's part, and he looked at them with a certain embarrassment.

'Come along! They can set another place . . .' said Maigret.

And he took his wife's arm across the esplanade. The young couple followed silently. Or rather Marie did the talking, in a low voice but in a firm manner.

'Do you know what she's saying to him?' the inspector asked his wife.

'Yes! She repeated it to me a dozen times over this morning to know whether it was all right. She's telling him that she doesn't mind about anything, *whatever may have happened.* . . . You see? She's not mentioning the woman. She's pretending she doesn't know, but she told me that all the same she would emphasize the words *whatever may have happened.* . . . Poor little thing! . . . She'd go to the ends of the earth for him.'

'Alas!' sighed Maigret.

'What do you mean?'

'Nothing. Is this our table?'

The lunch went quietly, too quietly. The tables were so close together that one could scarcely talk in an ordinary voice.

To put him at his ease, Maigret avoided looking at Le Clinche, but all the same the operator's behaviour worried him no less than it did Marie Léonnec, whose face was quite drawn.

Le Clinche remained mournful and dejected. He ate and drank and answered questions, but his thoughts were elsewhere. And several times, when he heard steps behind him, he started as if he thought he was in danger.

The bay windows of the dining-room were wide open and looked on to a sea spangled with sunshine. It was warm. Le Clinche was sitting with his back to the window, but every now and then he would turn round brusquely with a nervous movement, as if to interrogate the horizon.

Madame Maigret made conversation, chiefly addressing the girl, and uttering any commonplace so that the silence might not become oppressive.

The scene was not set for a tragedy – a family hotel, the comforting rattle of plates and glasses, on the table a half-bottle of claret and a bottle of mineral water.

74

The manager, misunderstanding the situation, came up at dessert and asked:

'Shall we get a room ready for the gentleman?'

He was looking at Le Clinche. He guessed he was the fiancé, and he probably took the Maigrets for the parents of the girl!

Two or three times the operator made the same gesture as he had made that morning during the identification, a rapid movement of his hand across his forehead. A feeble, weary gesture.

'What shall we do?'

The room was emptying. The four of them were standing on the terrace.

'Shall we sit down a little?' Madame Maigret proposed.

Their beach-chairs were still on the sand. The Maigrets sat down. The young people stood for a moment, rather embarrassed.

'Shall we go for a walk?' Marie Léonnec risked the suggestion with a vague smile in Madame Maigret's direction.

Left alone with his wife, the inspector lit a pipe and growled:

'I look for all the world like a prospective father-in-law!'

'They don't know what to do. It's a delicate situation ...' his wife remarked, following them with her eyes. 'Look at them. They're embarrassed. . . . I may be wrong, but I think Marie has more character than her fiancé ...'

It certainly was a pitiful sight to see that skinny figure walking listlessly along, taking no notice of his surroundings and, as one could guess from far off, saying nothing at all.

And yet one could see that Marie was making great efforts, chatting away to make him forget his troubles, even trying to appear gay.

There were other groups on the beach. But Le Clinche was the only man without white trousers. He was dressed for town, and that made him look more melancholy still.

'How old is he?' asked Madame Maigret.

And her husband, lying back in his deck-chair, his eyes half-closed, answered:

'Nineteen. He's only a boy... But I'm very much afraid that from now on he's a doomed man...'

'Why? Isn't he innocent?'

'He probably didn't do the murder. No! I'd swear to that. But I'm afraid that he's lost, all the same.... Look at him. Just look!'

'Nonsense! Once they're alone and have kissed each other...'

'Perhaps...'

Maigret was pessimistic.

'She's not much older than him. She's very fond of him. She's prepared to be a nice little wife...'

'Why do you think that...?'

'That it won't come off? Just an impression.... Have you ever looked at the photographs of people who died young? I have always been struck by the fact that those portraits, taken when the people were in good health, have already something melancholy about them. One might say that those destined to be the victims of a tragedy carry their doom on their faces...'

'And you find that this boy...?'

'Is a victim, and has always been a victim! He was born poor! He suffered from his poverty! He slaved away as best he could, desperately, like someone swimming against the current! He managed to get engaged to a charming girl in a social position superior to his. Well! I don't believe it.... Look at them. They're discussing things. They want to be optimistic. They're trying to believe in their future...'

Maigret talked quietly in a low tone while with his eyes he followed the two silhouettes outlined against the sparkling sea.

'Who is officially in charge of the case?'

'Girard, a superintendent at Le Havre. You don't know him. An intelligent man ...'

'Does he think he's guilty?'

'No! In any case, there's no proof, not even any serious presumptive evidence ...'

'What do *you* think?'

Maigret turned as if to look at the trawler which was hidden behind a block of houses.

'I think it was a fatal trip, for two men at least.... Fatal enough for Captain Fallut, when he came back, *not to be able to go on living*, and for the operator, *not to be able to take up the normal thread of his life again* ...'

'Because of a woman?'

He did not answer directly, but went on :

'And all the others, those who took no part in the tragedy, even the stokers, were branded by it, without their knowing. They came back surly, uneasy.... Two men and a woman for three months revolving round a deck-cabin.... Just a few black bulkheads pierced by port-holes.... That was all ...'

'I've seldom seen you so affected by a case. You talk of three people.... What could they have done? Something that was sufficient to kill Captain Fallut! ... And which is still sufficient to upset those two, who look as if they were searching on the beach for the fragments of their dreams ...'

They were coming back, their arms dangling, not knowing whether politeness required them to rejoin the Maigrets or discretion advised them to keep away.

In the course of their walk, Marie Léonnec had lost a great deal of her energy. She cast a discouraged look at

Madame Maigret. They could guess that all her attempts, all her spirits, had been hurled against a wall of despair or inertia.

*

Madame Maigret liked to have afternoon tea. So at four o'clock they all sat down on the hotel terrace under the striped parasols which lent an atmosphere of conventional gaiety to the scene.

Chocolate steamed in two cups. Maigret had ordered beer, Le Clinche brandy-and-water.

They were talking about Jorissen, the Quimper teacher who had summoned Maigret on behalf of the operator and brought Marie Léonnec to Fécamp. Banal phrases were being exchanged.

'He's the best man in the world . . .'

They were embroidering on this theme without conviction, because they had to say something. Suddenly Maigret blinked his eyes, which had been fastened on a couple coming along the esplanade.

It was Adèle and Gaston Buzier, he lounging along, his hands in his pockets, his straw hat on the back of his head, his walk nonchalant, she animated and provocative as usual.

'If only they don't notice us!' thought the inspector.

And, in that moment, Adèle's glance met his. She stopped and said something to her companion, who attempted to dissuade her.

Too late! She had crossed the road. One by one she examined the tables on the terrace, chose the one nearest the Maigrets, and sat down where she had Marie Léonnec right opposite her.

Her lover followed her with a shrug of his shoulders, touched his straw hat as he passed the inspector, and sat down astride a chair.

'What'll you have?'

'Not chocolate, anyway! A kümmel!'

Was that already a declaration of war? When she mentioned chocolate she fixed her eyes on Marie Léonnec's cup, and Maigret saw the girl start.

She had never seen Adèle. But she had understood. She looked at Le Clinche, who turned his head.

Madame Maigret's foot tapped her husband's twice.

'Should the four of us go on to the Casino? . . .'

She had guessed too. But nobody answered her. Only Adèle's voice came from the next table.

'What a heat!' she sighed. 'Take my jacket, Gaston . . .'

And she took off the jacket of her costume, revealing bare arms and a voluptuous figure in pink satin. Her eyes did not leave Marie Léonnec for a single moment.

'D'you like grey? Don't you think they ought to forbid people to wear such depressing colours at the seaside?'

It was madness! Marie Léonnec was in grey. Adèle showed she wanted to attack her anyhow, as quickly as possible.

'Well, waiter? Are you coming today?'

Her voice was shrill. It sounded as if she were intentionally exaggerating her vulgarity.

Gaston Buzier smelt danger. He knew his mistress. He said something to her in a low voice. But she answered loudly:

'Well? Isn't the terrace free for everybody?'

Madame Maigret was the only one who had her back turned. Maigret and the operator sat sideways to Adèle. Marie Léonnec was facing her.

'One person's as good as another! Only there are some people who come crawling at your feet when you can't bear the sight of them, and who don't even know you when they're in company! . . .'

And she laughed disagreeably. She stared at the girl, who turned crimson.

'How much is that, waiter?' asked Buzier, anxious to put an end to it.

'We've plenty of time! The same again, waiter! And bring me some peanuts . . .'

'We haven't any.'

'Well, go and get some. That's what you're paid for, isn't it?'

Two other tables were occupied. Looks were cast on the new couple, who could not pass unnoticed. Maigret was worried. He undoubtedly wanted to put an end to this scene, which threatened to turn out badly.

But, on the other hand, he had the operator before him, all palpitating under his eyes.

It was as exciting as a dissection. Le Clinche sat motionless. He had not turned towards the woman, but he could not help seeing her, however vaguely, on his left – in any case, the pink splash of her blouse.

His eyes were fixed, a leaden grey. And one hand, lying on the table, closed very, very slowly, like the tentacles of a sea-animal.

One could foresee nothing yet. Would he get up and flee? Would he throw himself on her as she went on talking? Would he . . . ?

No, none of these things. It was something quite different and a hundred times more moving. It was not only his hand that closed up, it was the whole man. He shrank and folded in on himself.

His eyes became the same grey as his skin.

He did not move. Did he even breathe? Not a tremor. But his motionlessness grew to nightmare intensity.

'This reminds me of another lover of mine, a married man with three children . . .'

Marie Léonnec, breathing quickly, swallowed her chocolate in a single gulp out of sheer embarrassment.

'. . . He was the world's most passionate man. Sometimes I would refuse to see him, and then he would sob on the landing and all the other lodgers would laugh their heads off. "My little Adèle, my adorable darling ..." The whole works you know! ... Well, one Sunday I met him out walking with his wife and kids. I heard his wife asking: "Who's that woman?" And he said, as solemn as a judge: "Some woman of the street, I expect! ... You can tell by the ridiculous way she's dressed ..." '

And she laughed. She was playing to the gallery and watching the effect of her behaviour on their faces.

'All the same, there are people who haven't much nerve ...'

Her companion again tried to silence her by saying something in a low voice.

'You go to hell! Have you got the willies? I pay for my drinks, don't I? ... I'm not doing anyone any harm! ... So they can't say anything to me.... What about those peanuts, waiter? And bring me another kümmel ...'

'Should we go? ...' said Madame Maigret.

It was too late. Adèle had got going. And they knew that if they went she would stop at nothing to make a scene.

Marie Léonnec stared at the table, her ears crimson, her eyes bright, her lips parted in anguish.

As for Le Clinche, he had closed his eyes, and thus he remained, blind, his face set. His hand still lay inert on the table.

Hitherto Maigret had had no chance of observing him in detail. His face was at once very young and very old, as is often the case with adolescents who have had a hard childhood.

He was tall, taller than the average, but his shoulders weren't yet a man's shoulders.

His skin, which was rather neglected, was sprinkled with clusters of freckles. He had not shaved that day, and the fair hairs gleamed on his chin and his cheeks.

He was not handsome. He could not have laughed much in his life. Instead, he had often burnt the midnight oil, read a great deal, written a great deal, in rooms without any fire, in his cabin jolted by the waves, by the light of miserable lamps.

'But what really makes me sick is when people pretend to be respectable when they're no better than the likes of us . . .'

Adèle was getting impatient. She was ready to say anything to attain her ends.

'Young girls, for instance, who pretend butter wouldn't melt in their mouths and who run after a man the way no tart would dare to . . .'

The proprietor of the hotel, from the doorstep, was trying to catch his customers' eyes to find out whether he ought to intervene.

Maigret saw only Le Clinche, close-up. His head was slightly bent forward. His eyes were still closed.

But tears spurted one by one from his closed lids, made their way through his lashes, paused and zigzagged down his cheeks.

It was not the first time the inspector had seen a man weep. But it was the first time he had ever been affected to such an extent, perhaps because of the silence, the immobility of the whole body.

Those fluid pearls were the only sign of life in the operator; the rest of him was dead.

Marie Léonnec had seen nothing. Adèle was just starting off again.

Then, a second later, Maigret had an intuition. The hand lying on the table unclenched itself imperceptibly. The other was in the pocket.

The eyelids opened a mere fraction of an inch, just enough to let a glimmer of a look filter through. And that look sought out Marie Léonnec.

Just as the inspector rose, a shot rang out and there was a general uproar and a scraping of chairs.

*

Le Clinche did not move immediately. Only his body drooped imperceptibly to the left, and his mouth opened in a faint rattle.

Marie Léonnec was slow in understanding because she had not seen the weapon. She threw herself on him, embraced his knees and his right hand, and turned to the inspector in desperation.

'Inspector! What is it? . . .'

Only Maigret had guessed. Le Clinche had a revolver in his pocket, obtained heaven knows where, because he had not had one when he came out of prison that morning.

And he had fired from his pocket! It was the butt-end that he had been clutching during those long minutes when Adèle was talking, while he closed his eyes, waiting and perhaps hesitating . . .

The bullet must have got him in the stomach or the side. One could see his burnt waistcoat, torn to ribbons as far as his hip.

'A doctor! . . . Police! . . .' someone cried.

A doctor, who had been on the beach a hundred yards from the hotel, came up in his bathing-suit.

They caught Le Clinche just as he fell, and carried him into the dining-room. Marie followed them like a woman demented.

Maigret had no time to bother with Adèle, or her lover. But as he was going into the café he saw her, livid, emptying down a large glass against which her teeth were chattering.

She had helped herself. She still had the bottle in her hand and she filled up the glass again . . .

The inspector did not look further, but somehow the

image of that pallid face above the pink bodice, and particularly the teeth chattering against the glass, remained in his mind.

He could not see Gaston Buzier. They were shutting the dining-room door.

'Please don't stay here . . .' the proprietor was requesting his guests. 'Keep calm! . . . The doctor wants as little noise as possible . . .'

Maigret pushed through the door and found the doctor on his knees. Madame Maigret was holding back the girl, who was making frantic efforts to throw herself on the injured man.

'Police . . .' Maigret whispered to the doctor.

'Can you get those ladies out of here? . . . I'll have to undress him and . . .'

'All right . . .'

'I'll need two people to help me. . . . They ought to phone for an ambulance straight away . . .'

He was still in his bathing-suit.

'Is it bad?'

'I can't say until the wound's been probed. . . . But you can see for yourself . . .'

Yes, Maigret could see for himself, a dreadful mess, flesh and rags of clothes all mixed up.

The tables were set for dinner. Madame Maigret went out, taking Marie Léonnec with her. A young man in flannel trousers came up and said timidly:

'Would you allow me to help you? I'm a medical student . . .'

An oblique ray of the sun, violently red, struck a window and was so blinding that Maigret went and let down the Venetian blind.

'Will you raise his legs? . . .'

He remembered what he had said to his wife that afternoon, comfortably installed in a deck-chair, following with his eyes that ungainly silhouette beside the smaller and livelier one of Marie Léonnec as they meandered along the shore.

'A doomed man . . .'

Captain Fallut had died the moment he got back. Pierre Le Clinche had struggled long and fiercely, perhaps he had still been struggling with his eyes shut, one hand on the table, the other in his pocket, while Adèle went on talking, talking and playing to the gallery.

8. The Drunken Sailor

It was shortly before midnight when Maigret came out of the hospital. He had waited to see the stretcher wheeled out of the operating-theatre bearing a muffled white form.

The surgeon was washing his hands. A nurse was setting the instruments in order.

'We'll try and save him!' he answered the inspector. 'The intestine is perforated in seven places. What one might call a dirty wound! We've cleared it all up . . .'

And he pointed to tubs full of blood, cotton-wool, and disinfectants.

'I can tell you it was a hell of a job . . .'

They were in excellent spirits, doctor, assistants, and nurses. When it had been brought in, the case had been as bad as it possibly could be, filthy, the stomach gaping open and burnt, with fragments of clothing encrusted in the flesh.

Now it was a clean body that was wheeled out on the stretcher. And the stomach was carefully sewn up.

The rest would come later. Perhaps Le Clinche would recover consciousness, perhaps not. At the hospital they did not even try to find out who he was.

'There's really a chance that he'll pull through?'

'Why not? I saw worse cases in the war . . .'

Maigret had immediately telephoned to the *Hôtel de la Plage* to reassure Marie Léonnec. Now he went off by himself. The hospital door closed behind him on its well-oiled hinges. It was night, the street with its little bourgeois houses was deserted.

He had not taken ten steps when a figure emerged from the shadow of a wall and Adèle's face was revealed in the light of a street-lamp.

'Is he dead?' she snapped at him

She must have been waiting for hours. Her face was drawn and the love-locks on her temples had lost their curl.

'Not yet!' Maigret answered in the same tone.

'Is he going to die?'

'Perhaps. . . . Perhaps not . . .'

'You believe I meant to do it?'

'I don't believe anything.'

'. . . because it's not true . . .'

The inspector walked on. She followed him and had to walk very quickly to keep up with him.

'You'll admit that at bottom it was his fault.'

Maigret pretended not to hear, but she persisted stubbornly.

'You know perfectly well what I mean. On board, he all but asked me to marry him. But once he was on shore . . .'

She wouldn't be put off. She seemed to be impelled by an irrepressible need to talk.

'If you think I'm a bad woman you don't know me. Only there are times . . . Listen to me, Inspector. . . . You must tell me the truth anyway. I know it was a bullet and that it got him point-blank in the stomach. . . . They've performed a laparotomy, haven't they?'

One could see that she had frequented hospitals, heard

doctors talking, and had been accustomed to people who had had more than one gunshot.

'Was the operation successful? It seems that it depends on what you had for your last meal . . .'

This was no violent show of emotion, just a harsh obstinacy that nothing could rebuff.

'Won't you answer me? And yet *you* knew why I carried on like that just now. Gaston's a rotter, I never loved him. . . . But this one . . .'

'There's a possibility that he'll live!' Maigret declared, looking the woman in the eyes. 'But, unless the mystery of the *Océan* is cleared up, it won't make much difference to him . . .'

He waited for a word, a shudder. She lowered her head.

'Of course you think I know . . . seeing that the two men were my lovers. And yet I swear. . . . No! You didn't know Captain Fallut. So you can't understand. He certainly was in love with me. He used to come and see me at Le Havre. And perhaps, at his age, a passion like that may have made him go a bit queer. But that made no difference to the fact that he was methodical in everything, very self-controlled, and quite mad the way he loved order. I still wonder how he could have made up his mind to hide me on board. . . . But what I do know is that we were hardly out to sea before he regretted it and began to detest me. His character changed quite suddenly . . .'

'But the operator hadn't seen you yet!'

'No! That wasn't until the fourth night, as I already told you . . .'

'Are you sure Fallut turned queer before then?'

'Not so much perhaps! But, later, there were days when it was quite like a nightmare, when I wondered whether he really hadn't gone mad . . .'

'And you haven't the slightest idea what might have

caused this behaviour?'

'No! I've thought about it. Sometimes I thought there was a secret between him and the operator ... I even thought they might be carrying contraband. Oh! nothing will persuade me to go on board a fishing-boat again! ... Consider that it went on for three months. And then the finish! ... One killed the moment we arrived. The other ... It is true that he's not dead, isn't it?'

They had come to the end of the quay, and the woman hung back.

'Where is Gaston Buzier?'

'At the hotel. He knows that it's no time to be bothering me and that for two pins I'd leave him ...'

'Are you going back to him?'

She shrugged her shoulders in a gesture which implied: 'Why not?'

A trace of her coquettish manner reappeared. As she left Maigret, she murmured with a strained smile:

'Thank you, Inspector. You've been very good to me. I ...'

She did not dare finish. But it was an invitation and a promise.

'All right! All right!' he growled as he hurried off.

And he pushed open the door of the *Rendez-Vous des Terre-Neuvas*.

*

With his hand on the handle he could hear quite clearly a confused noise from inside the café, as if about a dozen men were talking at once.

But as soon as the door was open, there was a complete silence, without any transition. And yet there were more than ten people in the room, in two or three groups, who must have been shouting across to each other from table to table.

The proprietor came up to Maigret and shook hands, not without a certain embarrassment.

'Is it true what they're saying, that Le Clinche has shot himself?'

His customers were suddenly very busy with their drinks. P'tit Louis was there, the Negro, the Breton, the chief engineer, as well as some others whom the inspector was beginning to know by sight.

'It's true!' said Maigret.

And he noticed that the chief engineer stirred uneasily on the bench, which was upholstered in oil-cloth.

'A fine trip!' growled a voice from one corner in a strong Norman accent.

And those words seemed to express the general opinion, for heads were nodded, a fist smote a marble table, and a voice echoed:

'Yes, an ill-fated trip!'

But Léon coughed to remind his clients to be discreet, and pointed at a sailor in a red blouse who was drinking alone.

Maigret went and sat down near the bar and ordered a brandy-and-soda.

There was no more conversation. Everyone was trying to put a good face on it. And Léon, skilful stage-manager, suggested to the largest group:

'Would you like a game of dominoes?'

It was one way of making a noise, of occupying their hands. The black dominoes were shuffled on the marble table. The proprietor sat down beside the inspector.

'I made them shut up,' he whispered, 'because that chap in the left-hand corner near the window is the kid's father. . . . You see?'

'What kid?'

'The cabin-boy ... Jean-Marie. The one who went overboard the third day out ...'

The man was listening. Although he couldn't catch the words he knew they were talking about him. He signed the barmaid to fill up his glass and he drank it off in one gulp, with a shudder of disgust.

He was already drunk. His bulging light-blue eyes were glassy. A wad of tobacco stuck out of his left cheek.

'Does he do Newfoundland too?'

'He used to. But now that he has seven children he fishes herring in winter because the trips are shorter; one month to begin with, and then getting shorter as the fish come south . . .'

'And in summer?'

'He fishes on his own, setting nets and lobster-pots . . .'

The man was on the same bench as Maigret, at the other end. But the inspector was watching him in a mirror.

He was short, broad-shouldered; the real Nordic sea-faring type, thick-set, plump, with no neck, pink skin, and fair hair. Like most fishers, his hands were covered with the scars of carbuncles.

'Does he always drink as much?'

'They all drink. . . . But it's specially since his kid died that he gets drunk. It gave him a turn to see the *Océan* again . . .'

But now the man was looking at them with an offended expression.

'What do you want with me?' he mumbled at Maigret.

'Nothing at all . . .'

All the sailors were following the scene without interrupting their game of dominoes.

'Because you'd better tell me! Perhaps I haven't the right to drink? . . .'

'Of course you have.'

'Tell me I haven't the right to drink . . .' he repeated with drunken obstinacy.

The inspector's eyes lighted on the black band he was wearing on his red blouse.

'Well, what do you both want, snooping round and talking about me?'

Léon signed to Maigret not to answer, but went up to his client.

'Come on now, no scenes, Canut. . . . It's not you the inspector's talking about, but this boy who's put a bullet in himself . . .'

'Serves him right! Is he dead?'

'No! . . . Perhaps they'll be able to save him . . .'

'Pity! I wish they were all dead! . . .'

Those words made a powerful impression. All faces were turned towards Canut. And he felt a need to shout louder:

'Yes, the whole lot of you!'

Léon was worried. He looked appealingly at everyone and made a hopeless gesture in Maigret's direction.

'Go on! Off to bed. . . . Your wife's waiting for you . . .'

'Go to hell!'

'Tomorrow you won't even have enough guts left to lift your nets . . .'

The drunken man sneered. P'tit Louis took the opportunity to call Julie.

'How much is that?'

'Are you paying for both rounds?'

'Yes, you can charge it to my account. I'll be getting my advance tomorrow before we sail . . .'

He rose automatically, imitated by the Breton, who followed his every step. He touched his cap. He did it again in Maigret's direction.

'Cowards!' growled the drunk as they went past him. 'They're all cowards . . .'

The Breton clenched his fists and nearly answered back, but P'tit Louis dragged him away.

'Go on off to bed . . .' said Léon again. 'Besides, we're closing . . .'

'I'll go when everyone else goes. I'm as good as anyone else, ain't I?'

And he looked at Maigret as if he wanted to provoke an argument.

'Look at that big man there . . . What's he up to?'

He was talking about the inspector. Léon was on hot coals. The last customers were waiting, convinced that something was going to happen.

'Oh, well! I might as well go. . . . How much?'

He fumbled under his blouse and brought out a leather pouch, threw some greasy notes on the table, rose to his feet, wobbled and got to the door, which he had great difficulty in opening.

He muttered something indistinctly, insults or threats.

When he got outside he pressed his face against the pane to give Maigret a last look; his nose was flattened on the misty glass.

'It gave him a turn . . .' said Léon, with a sigh as he went back to his place. 'He had only the one son. . . . All the other kids are girls and don't count, so to speak. . . .'

'What are they saying down here?' Maigret asked.

'About the operator? They don't know. So they invent. Stories about falling asleep standing . . .'

'What?'

'I don't know. It's still the *evil eye* . . .'

Maigret felt a keen look fixed on him. It was the chief engineer, who was sitting at the table just opposite.

'Has your wife got over her jealousy?' he asked him.

'Seeing that we're off tomorrow, I'd like to see her trying to keep me at Yport! . . .'

'The *Océan* sails tomorrow?'

'Yes, sails with the tide! Did you think the owners were going to let her rot in harbour?'

'They've found a captain?'

'A retired man who hasn't sailed for eight years! And what's more, he commanded a three-mast brig! It's going to be fun . . .'

'What about an operator?'

'They got a kid from school. . . . A Technical College they call it . . .'

'Is the second officer back?'

'They've wired him. He'll be here by morning . . .'

'And the crew?'

'It's always the same thing. They collect anyone hanging round the port. They'll always do, you know.'

'Have they got a cabin-boy?'

The other gave him a sharp look.

'Yes,' he said dryly.

'And you're glad to be going?'

No answer. The chief engineer ordered another grog. And Léon said in an undertone:

'They've just got news of the *Pacific*, which was due back this week. It's a ship of the same class as the *Océan*. In less than three weeks it had struck a rock and gone down. The whole crew is lost. I've got the wife of the second officer up there. She came from Rouen to meet her husband. She spends her whole time on the jetty. She knows nothing yet – the Company is awaiting confirmation before they publish the news . . .'

'A run of ill-luck!' growled the chief engineer, who had heard what he said.

The Negro yawned and rubbed his eyes, but did not dream of leaving. The abandoned dominoes made a complicated pattern on the grey rectangle of the table.

'In short,' said Maigret slowly, 'nobody knows why the operator tried to kill himself?'

His words met with an obstinate silence. Did all those men know? Did they carry even to this point the freemasonry of seafaring people who don't like to see landsmen interfering in their affairs?'

'What do I owe you, Julie?'

He rose, paid, and went heavily to the door. Ten pairs of eyes followed him. He turned, but met only sealed or scornful faces. Even Léon, in spite of all his goodwill, formed a united front with his clients.

The tide was out. Of the trawler, only the funnel and the derricks were to be seen. The trucks had disappeared. The quay was deserted.

A fishing-boat, its white light balanced on the top of the mast, was making slowly for the jetty, and one could hear two men's voices talking.

Maigret filled a last pipe, looked at the town, the Benedictine towers, with the gloomy walls of the hospital below.

The windows of the *Rendez-Vous des Terre-Neuvas* cast two rectangular pools of light on the quay.

The sea was calm. One only heard the faint murmur of the spring tide lapping at the shore and the piles of the jetty.

The inspector was right at the edge of the quay. Thick hawsers, the ones which held the *Océan,* were coiled round metal bollards.

He bent down. Men were closing down the hatchways of the holds where, during the day, they had stored the salt. A young man, even younger than Le Clinche, was standing watching the sailors at work, leaning against the operator's cabin.

It must be the successor to the man who had just put a bullet through his stomach. He was puffing away nervously at a cigarette.

He had come from Paris, from college. He was obviously excited. Perhaps he was dreaming of adventure.

Maigret couldn't tear himself away. He was kept there by the feeling that the mystery was quite near, within his reach, that there was only one more effort to be made ...

He turned suddenly, because he felt the presence of someone behind him. In the darkness he saw a red blouse, a black arm-band.

The man had not seen him, or else was paying no attention. He walked right up to the edge of the quay, and it was a miracle that, in his condition, he did not fall into space.

The inspector could see nothing but his back. He had the impression that, overcome by giddiness, the drunkard was going to throw himself on to the deck of the trawler.

But no! He was talking to himself, sneering and shaking his fist.

Then he spat once, twice, three times at the ship. He spat to express his complete disgust.

After which, no doubt having relieved his feelings, he went away, not towards his cottage in the fisher quarters, but towards the lower town where there might still be a light in some wretched little *bistro*.

9. Two Men on the Bridge

There was a tinny note from the direction of the cliff: the clock of the Benedictine abbey striking one.

Maigret walked towards the *Hôtel de la Plage*, his hands behind his back, but, as he got nearer, his steps became slower and finally stopped altogether, right in the middle of the quay.

Before him was the hotel, his room, his bed, everything that was peaceful and reassuring.

Behind ... He turned. He looked back at the funnel of the trawler from which smoke was coming gently, for the furnaces had been lit. Fécamp was asleep. There was a great pool of moonlight in the middle of the dock. A breeze had arisen from the water, almost icy, like the breath of the sea.

Maigret turned, heavily, regretfully. He again strode over the hawsers coiled round the bollards and found himself at the edge of the quay with his eyes fixed on the *Océan*.

His eyes were narrowed, his mouth threatening, his fists in the depths of his pockets.

This was the solitary, discontented Maigret, sunk within himself, doggedly persistent, caring nothing for ridicule.

The tide was low. The deck of the trawler far below the level of the dock. But a plank had been thrown from the quay to the bridge. A thin, narrow plank.

The sound of the surf was becoming more distinct. The tide must have turned, and the foamy water was gradually encroaching on the beach.

Maigret went on to the plank, which curved in the middle under his weight. His steps grated on the iron bridge. But he did not go any farther. He let himself down on the quarter-deck opposite the steering-wheel, where Captain Fallut's huge sea-mittens dangled from the compass.

In the same way dogs ensconce themselves, surly and obstinate, in a place where they have smelt out something.

The letter from Jorissen, his liking for Le Clinche, Marie Léonnec's importunity, were no longer his concern. This was a purely personal matter.

Maigret had reconstructed for himself the figure of Captain Fallut. He had made the acquaintance of the operator, of Adèle and the chief engineer. He had done his best to get the feel of the general life on board the trawler.

And yet this wasn't enough, something eluded him, he had the impression that he understood everything but the very essence of the drama.

Fécamp was asleep. On board, the sailors were in their bunks. The inspector rested his full weight on the quarter-deck, his back rounded, his knees slightly apart, his elbows on his knees.

And here and there his glance collected some detail: the gloves, for instance, huge, shapeless, worn by Fallut only when he was on watch, and left there by him. . . . By turning half round he could see the poop. In front of him he could see the whole bridge, the fo'c's'le and, quite near, the radio-room.

The water slapped the sides of the ship, which was imperceptibly getting up steam. And now that the furnaces were lit and the boilers filled with water, the ship seemed much more alive than on the previous days.

Was P'tit Louis sleeping down below beside heaps of coal?

On the right was a lighthouse. At the end of one jetty was a green light: a red one at the end of the other. The sea was a great black hole which gave out a strong smell.

It wasn't exactly an effort of thought that Maigret was making, but slowly and ponderously he took everything in, trying to feel the setting, to bring it to life. And gradually he worked himself into a sort of feverish condition.

'It was on such a night as this – colder, because spring had scarcely begun . . .

'The trawler was in the same place, a thread of smoke coming from the funnel, a few men sleeping below.

'Pierre Le Clinche at Quimper had dined with his fiancée in the family circle. Marie Léonnec had probably seen him to the door to give him a kiss.

'Then he had sped through the night in a third-class compartment. He would be back in three months. He would see her again. . . . Then another trip, and in winter, round about Christmas, they would get married . . .

'He didn't sleep. His kitbag was up on the rack. . . . In it were the provisions his mother had prepared . . .

'At the same time Captain Fallut was coming out of the little house in the Rue d'Etretat where Madame Bernard was sleeping.

'He was probably very nervous and worried, tortured in advance by remorse. Wasn't there a tacit understanding that some day he would marry his landlady?

'But all winter he had been going to Le Havre, as often as several times a week, to see a woman! A woman whom he didn't dare to show in Fécamp! A woman he was keeping! Who was young, pretty, and desirable, but whose vulgarity was rather disturbing.

'A good, orderly, meticulous man. A model of probity, whom the owners cited as an example and whose ship's papers were real masterpieces of detail!

'And now, all alone, he was going through the sleeping streets to meet her train at the station. Did he still hesitate?

'But three months! Would he find her again when he came back? Wasn't she far too fond of life to remain faithful to him? . . .

'She was quite a different type from Madame Bernard! She did not spend her time arranging her house, polishing her brasses and her floors, and building up plans for the future . . .

'No! She was a woman whose image in his mind made him blush and breathe faster.

'There she was! She laughed with a shrill laugh, just as provocative as her flesh! It would be fun to go on a ship, to be hidden on board, to have a real adventure.

'Shouldn't he warn her that the adventure mightn't be such fun? That, on the contrary, being shut up in a cabin during a three months' trip might be deadly?

'He swore he would tell her – but he did not dare! Once she was there, laughing and swelling out her breast, he was incapable of talking sense.

' "You're going to smuggle me on board secretly, tonight?"

'They set off. In the cafés and at the *Rendez-Vous des Terre-Neuvas* the fishers were going on the binge with the advance they had been paid that afternoon.

'And Captain Fallut, small and natty, grew paler as he approached the harbour and his ship. He could see the funnel. His throat was dry. Wasn't there still time? ...

'But Adèle was hanging on his arm. He could feel her, warm and trembling, against his flank.'

*

And Maigret, turning towards the empty quay, tried to imagine the two of them.

'Is that your ship? What a queer smell it has! Have we got to cross this plank?'

They went across. Captain Fallut anxiously told her to keep quiet.

'Is that the wheel you steer by?'

'Sh! ...'

They went down the iron ladder. They were on the bridge. They went into the captain's cabin and shut the door.

'Yes! That was it!' Maigret growled. 'There they were, the two of them. It was their first night on board ...'

He would have liked to tear aside the curtain of the night and disclose the wan light of dawn, see the silhouettes of the sailors staggering along, loaded with liquor, to join the ship.

The chief engineer arrived from Yport by the first morning train. The second officer came from Paris, Le Clinche from Quimper.

The men moved about the deck, argued about bunks

in the fo'c's'le, laughed, changed their clothes, and reappeared encased in stiff oilskins.

Then there was the new cabin-boy, Jean-Marie, who had come holding his father's hand. They jostled him around, teasing him about his boots, which were too big for him, and the tears that came so readily to his eyes.

The captain was still in his cabin. At last the door opened. He closed it carefully behind him. He looked dried up and very pale, with a drawn face.

'You're the operator? Good! I'll give you your instructions immediately. . . . In the meantime, take a look at the radio.'

Time passed. The owner was on the quay. Wives and mothers were still bringing parcels for the departing men.

Fallut trembled at the thought of the cabin whose door must not be opened at any price, for Adèle, half-undressed, her mouth open, was lying across the bed, asleep.

Everyone felt a slight early morning nausea, not only Fallut, but the men who had been doing the rounds of all the pubs in the town, and the ones who had come by train.

One by one they dropped into the *Rendez-Vous des Terre-Neuvas* and gulped down coffee laced with rum.

'Au revoir! If we get back . . .!'

There was a loud siren blast, then two more. The women and children, after a last embrace, ran towards the jetty. The owner shook hands with Fallut.

The hawsers were cast loose. The trawler slipped away from the quay. . . . Then Jean-Marie, the cabin-boy, overcome by fear, burst into sobs, stamped his feet and tried to jump ashore.

Fallut had stood where Maigret stood now.

'Stand by! A hundred and fifty degrees! ... Half-speed ahead!'

Was Adèle still asleep? Would she hate being upset by the first swell?

Fallut did not move from the post which had been his for so many years. Before him lay the sea, the Atlantic....

All his nerves were on edge with this mad thing he had done. It had not seemed so bad on shore.

'Two points to port ...'

And then there were cries and the group of people on the jetty surged forward! A man who had climbed up the derrick to wave good-bye to his people had fallen on to the deck!

'Stop! Hard-astern. Stop! ...'

Nothing stirred from the direction of the cabin.... Was there still time to put the woman back on shore? ...

Boats approached. The ship came to a standstill between the jetties. A fishing-smack wanted to get past.

But the man was injured and must be left behind. He was taken off in a dory ...

The superstitious women on shore were quite overcome by the accident. And the cabin-boy, in addition, was so afraid of going that he had to be held back from throwing himself into the water! ...

'Stand by! ... Half-speed! ... Full speed ahead! ...'

Le Clinche was taking possession of his domain, trying the gear, ear-phones on his head. And in the midst of his duties he wrote:

My darling sweetheart,
Eight o'clock in the morning! We are just off.... Already the town is out of sight ...

Maigret lit another pipe and rose so as to see his surroundings better. He had all his characters in hand, he had them all moving in their appointed places on the ship which he surveyed.

The first breakfast in the narrow cabin reserved for officers: Fallut, the second officer, the chief engineer, and the operator. And the captain announced that he would take his meals alone in his cabin . . .

It was something unheard of! A fantastic idea! Everyone tried vainly to think what could be the reason.

And Maigret, his head in his hand, went on muttering:

'It was the cabin-boy's duty to carry up the captain's food. And the captain would either have to open the door a very small way or to hide Adèle under the bed which he had raised up . . .'

There were two of them to eat a single portion! The first time, the woman laughed! And Fallut probably gave nearly the whole of his share to her.

He was too serious. She laughed at him. She coaxed him. . . . He yielded and smiled . . .

Had they already begun to talk of the evil eye in the fo'c's'le? . . . Weren't there comments on the captain's decision to eat alone? And besides, they had never known a captain who went about with the key of his cabin in his pocket!

The two propellers revolved. The vibrations had started which would shake the ship for the next three months.

Down below, men like P'tit Louis were feeding the furnaces with coal eight or ten hours a day, or sleepily examining the oil-pressure . . .

Three days. . . . That was the general opinion. . . . It had needed three days to produce an atmosphere of uneasiness. . . . And from that time the men had wondered whether Fallut had gone mad.

Why? Was it jealousy? But Adèle had declared that she hadn't seen Le Clinche until the fourth day . . .

Up to then he had been too busy with his apparatus.

He intercepted messages for his own personal satisfaction. He made attempts at transmission. And, the earphones on his head, he wrote pages and pages as if the post would carry them immediately to his fiancée.

Three days. They would hardly have had time to make each other's acquaintance. Perhaps the chief engineer had pressed his face against the port-hole and seen the young woman? But he had said nothing!

The atmosphere on board ship is only created gradually, as men get nearer to each other by sharing their adventures in common. But as yet there were no adventures! They hadn't even begun fishing! For that they would have to wait until they were on the Great Bank over there in Newfoundland, on the other side of the Atlantic, which they wouldn't reach for at least ten days.

*

Maigret was standing up there on the bridge, and if a man had wakened up he might have wondered what he was doing there, enormous, solitary, looking slowly round him.

What was he doing? He was trying to understand! All the people were in their places, with their own particular mentalities and their own particular preoccupations.

But from then on there was no way of guessing. There was nothing but a blank. The inspector could only review the evidence.

'It was by about the third day that Captain Fallut and the operator had come to regard each other as enemies. They both kept revolvers in their pockets. They seemed to be afraid of each other . . .'

And yet Le Clinche had not yet become Adèle's lover!

'From then onwards, the captain acted like a madman . . .'

They were out in the Atlantic now, off the route of steamers. They only very occasionally met other trawlers, English or German, on their way to their fishing-grounds.

Was Adèle getting impatient and complaining about her life of confinement?

'... *like a madman* ...'

Everyone was agreed on that word! And it would seem as if Adèle weren't sufficient to produce such a state of mind in a man as balanced as Fallut, a man who all his life had worshipped orderliness.

She hadn't been unfaithful to him! He had let her have two or three airings on the bridge at night, taking all manner of precautions.

Then why was he *like a madman*? ...

The evidence continued:

'... He gave orders to anchor the boat where no cod had ever been caught within living memory ...'

And he wasn't a nervous or a fiery or hasty man! He was a meticulous *petit bourgeois* who had once dreamed of uniting himself with his landlady, Madame Bernard, and ending his days in the house in the Rue d'Etretat with its lace curtains.

'... Accidents went on happening. ... When they finally reached the Bank and found some fish, it was salted in such a way that it was considerably damaged by the time they got back.'

Fallut was no beginner. He was due to retire! No one had ever had anything against him before.

He always ate in his cabin.

'... He sulked with me ...' Adèle had said. 'He'd let days and weeks go past without saying a word to me. Then suddenly it would get hold of him again ...'

A wave of sensuality! She was there, in his room! Sharing his bed! And yet he managed to leave her alone for weeks, until the temptation became too strong!

Would he have acted like that if he had only been troubled by jealousy?

The chief engineer prowled, fascinated, round the cabin, but hadn't the nerve to pick the lock.

Then the epilogue: the return of the *Océan* to France with a cargo of damaged cod.

It must have been on the way back that the captain drew up that sort of will in which he declared that no one must be accused of his death.

Therefore he wanted to die! He wanted to kill himself! Nobody but he was capable of taking the bearings, and he was sufficiently imbued with the sailor's code to bring his ship back into port first.

Would he have killed himself because he had broken the regulations by taking a woman with him? Would he have killed himself because the oversalted fish would have to be sold at a few francs below the current price?

Would he have killed himself because his crew, astonished by his strange behaviour, thought he had gone mad?

He, the coolest and most meticulous captain in Fécamp? Whose ship's papers were cited as a model? Who had lived so long in Madame Bernard's placid house?

The ship came alongside. All the men jumped off and made for the *Rendez-Vous des Terre-Neuvas*, where they could at last get a drink of spirits.

They were all branded with the seal of the mystery! They were all silent about certain things! They were all uneasy!

Because the captain had behaved in an inexplicable manner?

Fallut came ashore quite alone. He would have to wait until the quays were deserted to take off Adèle.

He walked a few steps. Two men were hiding: the operator and Gaston Buzier, the woman's lover.

But that did not prevent a third man from leaping on

the captain, strangling him and pushing him into the dock.

*

And that had happened in the very place where the *Océan* was now floating in the black water. The body had caught on the chain of the anchor . . .

Maigret smoked, his brow set.

'At his first interrogation, Le Clinche lied and talked about a man with yellow shoes who had killed Fallut. . . . The man with the yellow shoes was Buzier. . . . Confronted with him, Le Clinche withdrew his statement . . .'

Why did he lie, unless to save the third person, that is to say, the murderer? And why wouldn't Le Clinche reveal his name?

Far from it! He let himself be imprisoned in his place! He scarcely defended himself when there was every chance that he would be found guilty!

He was gloomy, like a man eaten up with remorse. He did not dare look his fiancée or Maigret in the eyes.

And one tiny detail: before he returned to the trawler he went to the *Rendez-Vous des Terre-Neuvas* and, upstairs in his room, he burned his papers . . .

When he got out of prison he was quite joyless, even when Marie Léonnec was there, urging him to be optimistic. . . . And he found a way of getting hold of a revolver . . .

He was afraid. . . . He hesitated. . . . For a long time he had remained with his eyes closed and his fingers on the trigger . . .

Then he had fired . . .

*

As the night wore on the air became cooler and the breeze more charged with the musty smell of seaweed and iodine.

The trawler had risen a few feet. The bridge was now

on a level with the quay, and the suction of the tide made it lurch sideways and caused the gangway to creak.

Maigret had forgotten his fatigue. The worst hour had passed. Day was near.

He drew up a list:

Captain Fallut, who had been taken off the anchor-chain, dead.

Adèle and Gaston Buzier, who were always quarrelling, fed up with each other and yet with no one else to turn to.

Le Clinche, who had been wheeled out on a stretcher, swathed in white, from the operating-theatre.

And Marie Léonnec.

And those men who, even when they were drunk, at the *Rendez-Vous des Terre-Neuvas*, remembered something terrible.

'The third day!' said Maigret aloud. 'That's where we'll have to look! Something happened more terrifying than jealousy. *And yet something which was a direct result of the presence of Adèle on board . . .*'

The effort was painful. There was a tension in all his faculties. The ship swayed imperceptibly. There was a light in the fo'c's'le where the sailors were getting up.

'The third day . . .'

Then his throat tightened. He looked at the quarter-deck and then at the quay where lately a man had stooped down and shaken his fist.

Perhaps it was the effect of the cold. In any case, a shudder passed over him.

The third day. The cabin-boy . . . Jean-Marie, who had stamped his foot and hadn't wanted to go . . . and was washed overboard by a wave . . . in the night . . .

Maigret stared round the deck as if trying to find the exact place where the catastrophe had occurred.

There were only two witnesses, Captain Fallut and

the operator, Le Clinche. The next day, or the day after, Le Clinche became Adèle's lover . . .

It was a clean break. Maigret didn't wait an instant longer. Someone was moving in the fo'c's'le. Without being seen, he crossed the plank which connected the ship with the land.

And, lugubriously, his hands in his pockets, his nose blue with the cold, he went back to the *Hôtel de la Plage*.

It wasn't yet day, but it was no longer night, for on the sea the crests of the waves loomed up, crudely white. And the seagulls made light splashes on the sky.

A train whistled in the station. An old woman went off towards the rocks, her basket on her back, a hooked stick in her hand, to catch crabs.

10. What Happened on the Third Day

When Maigret came down from his room at about eight in the morning he felt light in the head and heavy in the chest, as if he had been drinking too much.

'Isn't it going as it should?' his wife asked him.

He shrugged his shoulders and she did not press him. But there on the hotel terrace, facing a treacherous green sea breaking into white horses, he came upon Marie Léonnec. She was not alone. There was a man sitting at her table. She rose precipitately and stammered out:

'Allow me to introduce you to my father, who has just arrived.'

The wind was fresh, the sky overcast. The seagulls were skimming low over the water.

'I am most honoured, Inspector. Most honoured and most happy . . .'

Maigret looked mournfully at him. He was short on his legs and would have been no more ridiculous than anyone else had it not been for a disproportionate nose, as big as two or three ordinary ones, pitted, moreover, like a strawberry.

It wasn't his fault! It was a genuine infirmity. But that made no difference to the fact that one saw nothing but the nose, and when he talked, one looked only at the nose, which made it impossible to take seriously anything he might say.

'You'll have a drink with us?'

'No, thank you. I've just had breakfast.'

'Well, a little brandy to warm you up.'

'Don't bother!'

But he insisted. It was only polite, wasn't it, to make people drink against their wills?

And Maigret observed him and his daughter, who, apart from the nose, was very like him. Looking at her in this way, he could see pretty well what she would be like in about ten years, when the charm of youth had gone.

'I want to go straight to the point, Inspector. That's my motto. I've travelled all night for this. When Jorissen came and told me that he would accompany my daughter, I gave my permission. So no one can say I'm not broadminded...'

If only Maigret hadn't been in a hurry to go somewhere else! And there was that nose! And a certain vulgarity which came out in his conversation.

'Nevertheless, my duty as a father compels me to find out what's what, doesn't it? That's why I ask you, out of your goodness of heart, to tell me whether you think that the young man is innocent...'

Marie Léonnec looked away. She must have felt confusedly that this interference of her father wasn't going to settle anything.

Alone, running to the rescue of her fiancé, she had a certain charm. At least she was touching.

But seen with her family it was different. It was too suggestive of the shop at Quimper, the discussions before her departure, the gossiping neighbours.

'You're asking me whether he killed Captain Fallut?'

'Yes. . . . You'll understand that it is essential.'

Maigret looked straight in front of him with his most distant expression.

'Well . . .'

He could see that the girl's hands were trembling.

'He didn't kill him. You'll excuse me . . . I have most urgent business. I expect I'll have the pleasure of seeing you again quite soon.'

He fled! He even upset a chair on the terrace. He could guess that they were struck all of a heap, but he did not look round to see.

On the quay he kept to the pavement, away from the *Océan*. But he could not help noticing that some men had just arrived with their kitbags on their shoulders, and were taking a look round the ship. A cart was unloading sacks of potatoes. The owner was there with his patent-leather boots and his pencil behind his ear.

There was a lot of noise coming from the *Rendez-Vous des Terre-Neuvas* and the door was open. Maigret could just make out P'tit Louis holding forth to a group of the new hands.

He did not stop. He hastened his steps as he saw the proprietor making signs to him. Five minutes later, he was ringing the bell at the door of the hospital.

*

The assistant was quite young. Under his overall his suit was in the latest fashion, his tie was exquisite.

'The radio operator? I took his pulse and his temperature this morning. He's doing as well as is to be expected . . .'

'His mind's quite clear?'

'Oh, yes, I think so. He's said nothing to me, but he keeps following me with his eyes . . .'

'Can I talk to him about serious matters?'

The assistant made a vague gesture of indifference.

'I don't see why not. Once the operation's successfully over and the temperature's normal . . . Would you like to see him?'

Pierre Le Clinche was alone in a little enamelled room kept at a moist heat. He watched Maigret come up, and his eyes were clear and untroubled.

'You see, he couldn't be doing better. . . . He'll be up in a week. But, on the other hand, there's a possibility that he'll limp, because one of the tendons on the thigh has been severed. And he'll have to take certain precautions. . . . Would you prefer to be left alone with him?'

It was slightly embarrassing. The day before, it was a real bundle of rags that had been brought in, bleeding and filthy. One would have sworn there wasn't a breath of life left in him.

And now Maigret found a white bed, a face that was slightly drawn, a little pale, but more peaceful than he had ever seen it. It was almost serenity that one read in those eyes.

That is perhaps why he hesitated. He marched up and down the room, pressed his forehead a moment against the double window from which one could see the harbour and the trawler with the men working in red jerseys.

'Do you feel strong enough to have a talk?' he growled suddenly, turning towards the bed.

Le Clinche made a faint sigh of assent.

'You know that I'm not officially connected with this case? My friend Jorissen asked me to prove your innocence. Well, that's done! You didn't kill Captain Fallut . . .'

Maigret heaved a great sigh. Then he got on with it and went straight to the point.

'Tell me the truth about what happened on the third day, that's to say, about the death of Jean-Marie.'

He avoided looking the sick man in the face. He filled a pipe for something to do, and as the silence seemed as if it would last for ever, he murmured :

'It was evening. There were only you and Captain Fallut on the bridge. . . . Were you together?'

'No! . . .'

'Was the captain walking near the poop?'

'Yes. I had just come out of my cabin. . . . He didn't see me. . . . I watched him, because I thought there was something queer about his conduct . . .'

'You didn't know yet that there was a woman on board?'

'No! I thought rather that, as he closed his door so carefully, he must have some contraband articles in his room . . .'

His voice was weary. And yet it rose as he exclaimed :

'It is the most frightful thing I have ever known, Inspector. . . . But who has been talking? Tell me . . .'

He closed his eyes as he had closed them when he was waiting to fire a bullet into his stomach from his pocket.

'Nobody. The captain was walking up and down, nervously, I imagine, as he had been since you sailed. . . . But there was someone at the helm, I suppose? . . .'

'A steersman! But he couldn't see us, in the darkness . . .'

'Then the cabin-boy turned up . . .'

He was interrupted by Le Clinche half-raising himself with his hands clutching at the ropes which hung from the ceiling to facilitate his movements.

'Where is Marie?'

'At the hotel. Her father has just come . . .'

'To take her away! That's good! . . . He ought to take her away. . . . And above all, she mustn't come here! . . .'

He was working himself up to a fever. His voice was duller, his utterance jerky.

One could see that his temperature was rising. His eyes grew brighter.

'I don't know who's been talking. . . . But now I must tell you everything . . .'

He was so wildly excited that it almost seemed as if he were in a delirium.

'A most extraordinary thing. . . . You didn't know the kid. . . . Quite skinny. . . . And dressed in clothes cut down from one of his father's old suits. . . . The first day he was frightened and he cried. . . . How can I explain? . . . Afterwards he made up for it by dirty tricks. It was only to be expected at his age. . . . But you know what I mean by a *dirty-minded kid*. . . . He was one. . . . Twice I caught him reading letters I had written to my fiancée . . . And he just said impudently: "Is that your skirt?"

'That evening . . . I expect the captain was walking up and down because he was too nervous to sleep. . . . The sea was pretty choppy. . . . Every now and then a big wave would come over the side and wet the deck-plates. . . .

'I was perhaps ten yards away. . . . I only heard a few words. . . . But I could see their figures. . . . The kid swanking and laughing. . . . The captain with his head sunk in his jersey and his hands in his pockets. . . .

'Jean-Marie had talked to me of "my skirt". . . . He must have been teasing even Fallut. . . . He had a shrill voice. . . . I remember catching the words: "And if I told everyone that . . ."

'I only understood afterwards. . . . It was he who had discovered that the captain had a woman hidden in his cabin. . . . He was quite proud about it. . . . He thought he was smart. . . . He was bad without knowing it . . .

'Then this is what happened. . . . The captain made a movement as if he'd hit him. . . . The kid, who was very

113

quick, dodged the blow and shouted something which must have been another threat that he'd talk ...

'Fallut's hand struck a stay. . . . It must have hurt him and made him mad with rage ...

'It was like the fable of the lion and the gnat. . . . He forgot his dignity and began chasing the kid, who ran away, laughing at first. But gradually he got panicky. . . .

'There was a chance that someone might hear and understand immediately what it was all about. . . . Fallut was crazy with anxiety ...

'I saw him make a grab at Jean-Marie's shoulders, but, instead of laying hold of him, he pushed him forward ...

'That's all. . . . Accidents will happen. . . . His head struck a capstan. . . . I heard something frightful – a sort of dull thud. . . . *It was his skull* . . .'

*

He passed his hands across his face. He was livid. Sweat was pouring from his forehead.

'At this point a wave swept the deck. . . . So that the figure was already soaked when the captain bent over. . . . At the same moment he saw me. . . . Probably I'd forgotten to keep hidden. . . . I took a few steps forward. . . . I came up in time to see the body of the boy crumple up and then stiffen in a way I shall never forget. . . .

'He was dead. . . . Senselessly! . . . And we stood staring at each other without understanding, without realizing this frightful thing ...

'No one had seen or heard anything. . . . Fallut didn't dare touch the child. . . . It was I who examined his chest, his hands, and his cracked skull. . . . There was no blood. . . . No wound. . . . Only the skull was bashed in ...

'We must have spent about a quarter of an hour there, not knowing what to do, miserable, our shoulders frozen, with the spray occasionally dashing in our faces ...

'The captain was a different man. You would have thought that something had cracked in him too . . .

'When he spoke, it was in a cold, incisive voice: "The crew mustn't know the truth! For the sake of discipline!"

'And it was he who, in my presence, lifted up the boy. There was only one thing to do.... Wait! I remember that with his thumb he made the sign of the cross on his forehead ...

'Twice the sea hurled the body against the hull. We were still standing there in the darkness. We didn't dare look at each other. We didn't dare speak ...'

Maigret had just lit a pipe and was gripping the stem hard with his teeth.

A nurse came in. The two men turned such absent-minded eyes on her that she stammered out in embarrassment:

'I just came to take his temperature ...'

'In a minute!'

As the door closed the inspector murmured:

'It was then he spoke to you of his mistress?'

'From that time he was never the same again.... I don't think he was really mad.... But there was something wrong.... He started by touching me on the shoulder ...

' "All because of a woman, young man! ...." he murmured.

'I was cold and yet feverish. I couldn't help looking at the sea on the side where the body had been thrown over ...

'You've heard what the captain was like? A dry, little man with an energetic expression. He talked rapidly in short unfinished sentences ...

' "There you are! Fifty-five years old. Nearly retired. A solid reputation. Saved a bit. Now I'm finished! Done for! In a minute! In less than a minute. Because of a kid who . . . Or rather because of a woman . . ."

'And so, in the night, in a dull and angry voice, he told me everything, bit by bit. . . . A woman from Le Havre. . . . A woman who was pretty worthless, he realized that. . . . But he couldn't get over her . . .

'He had taken her on board. . . . At the same time he had the feeling that her presence would provoke trouble . . .

'She was there . . . asleep . . .'

He moved restlessly.

'I don't remember everything he told me. . . . For he felt he had to talk about her – with a mixture of passion and hatred . . .

'"A captain has no right to start a scandal capable of ruining his authority . . ."

'I can still hear those words. It was the first time I'd sailed on a ship, and now I thought of the sea as a monster that would get us all . . .

'Fallut cited examples. In such and such a year a captain had taken his mistress with him on his ship. There had been such rows on board that three men hadn't come back . . .

'It was blowing hard. . . . Spray kept dashing over us. . . . Sometimes a wave would lick round our feet, which slipped about on the greasy metal deck . . .

'No, he wasn't mad! . . . But it wasn't the same Fallut . . .

'"We'll get this trip over! . . . Then we'll see . . ."

'I didn't understand what he meant. It seemed to me both conventional and fantastic to be so attached to the idea of duty.

'"They mustn't know. . . . A captain must do no wrong . . ."

'I was ill with nerves. I couldn't think. Thoughts were going round and round in my head, and finally I was living in a real nightmare.

'This woman in the cabin, this woman whom a man like the captain couldn't get over ... whose very name made him breathe fast ...

'I wrote scores of letters to my fiancée, but we were going to be separated for three months. ... I had had no experience of such transports ...

'And when he said *her flesh* ... or *her body* ... I blushed without knowing why ...'

Maigret questioned him slowly:

'No one on board except you two knew the truth about the death of Jean-Marie?'

'No one!'

'And it was the captain who, in accordance with tradition, recited the prayers for the dead?'

'At dawn. The weather had broken. We ran into an icy mist ...'

'The crew said nothing?'

'There were some queer looks and whispers. But Fallut was more wilful than ever and his voice had become quite mordant. He didn't permit of the least reply. He got angry merely if a man's expression didn't please him. He spied on the men as if he was trying to guess whether any suspicions could have arisen ...'

'And you?'

Le Clinche did not reply. He stretched out his arm to reach a glass of water which stood on the bedside table, and drank greedily.

'You prowled round the cabin more than ever, didn't you? You wanted to see this woman who'd put the captain in such a state? ... Was that on the following night? ...'

'Yes ... I met her for a moment. Then the next night ... I had noticed that the key to the radio-room and the captain's cabin were the same. ... The captain was on watch. ... I crept in like a thief ...'

'You became her lover? ...'

117

The operator's face hardened.

'I swear you won't understand! The whole atmosphere had no connexion whatsoever with everyday realities. That kid ... And the whole business of the previous night.... And yet, when I thought of it, it was always the same image that came to my mind: that of a woman different from all other women, a woman whose body, whose flesh could so change a man ...'

'Did she encourage you?'

'She was lying on the bed, half-naked ...'

He blushed violently and turned away his head.

'How long did you remain in the cabin?'

'Perhaps two hours ... I don't know. When I came out there was a buzzing in my ears and the captain was at the door. He said nothing.... He watched me go past. I nearly threw myself on my knees and cried out that it wasn't my fault and begged his forgiveness. But his face was frozen. I walked off ... back to my post.

'I was afraid.... From then on I kept my revolver loaded in my pocket, because I was convinced he was going to kill me ...

'He never spoke a word to me except on matters of routine. What's more, most of the time he sent me written instructions ...

'I wish I could explain it better ... I just can't. Each day was worse than the last. I had the impression that everyone knew about the tragedy.

'The chief engineer began haunting the cabin too, and the captain would spend hours shut up inside.

'The men kept giving us anxious, inquiring looks.... They guessed that something was up. Hundreds of times I heard them talking of the evil eye ...

'And I had only one desire ...'

'Naturally!' growled Maigret.

There was a silence, and Le Clinche fixed reproachful eyes on the inspector.

'There was filthy weather for the next ten days. I was sick. But I kept thinking of her. She had scent on. She . . . I can't tell you! . . . It made me ill! Yes! It was the kind of desire that made you ill, made you cry with rage! . . . Especially when I saw the captain going into the cabin! Because now I imagined things. . . . You know – she had called me her *big boy* . . . in a special kind of a voice, rather husky! And I used to repeat those words over again to torture myself. . . . I stopped writing to Marie. . . . I indulged in impossible dreams of going off with this woman as soon as we got back to Fécamp . . .'

'And the captain?'

'He became still more icy, more cutting. Perhaps, after all, it was insanity in his case . . . I don't know. He ordered them to fish in a certain place, and all the old sailors swore that no fish had ever been seen in those latitudes. . . . He wouldn't allow them to say a word! He was afraid of me. I don't know whether he knew I was armed. He was armed too. When we met, his hand would go to his pocket. I tried hundreds of times to see Adèle again. But he was always there! With shadows round his eyes and his lips drawn back! And the smell of cod. . . . The men were salting the cod in the hold. . . . There was one accident after another.

'The chief engineer kept hanging round too. And we were no longer talking to one another. We were like three madmen. There were nights when I thought I would have killed someone to get back to her. Can you understand that? Nights when I tore my handkerchief with my teeth while I repeated to myself, in her voice:

' "*My big boy! . . . Big stupid! . . .*"

'And it was so long! Days followed nights, and then more days! With nothing but the grey water round us, cold fogs, and the scales and entrails of cod everywhere . . .

'The nauseating taste of brine in one's throat . . .

119

'And nothing but that one time! I believe if I could have only been with her one other time I should have been cured! But it was impossible. He was there! He was always there, and the shadows round his eyes grew blacker . . .

'And that perpetual rolling, that life without a horizon. Then we saw cliffs again . . .

'Can you imagine that going on for three months? . . . Well! Instead of being cured I was even more ill. It is only now that I realize it was an illness . . .

'I detested the captain, who was always in my way. I had a horror of this old man shutting himself up with a woman like Adèle . . .

'I was afraid of getting back to port. I was afraid of losing her for ever . . .

'In the end I thought of him as a sort of demon! Yes, a kind of malevolent spirit who kept the woman for himself . . .

'The boat was badly handled as we came into port. Then the men leapt ashore with relief and made a rush for the pubs. I knew, of course, that the captain was only waiting for nightfall to let Adèle out.

'I went to my room at Léon's. There were some old letters and photos of my fiancée there, and, I don't know why, overcome with fury I burned them all . . .

'I came out. I wanted her! . . . I tell you, I wanted her! Hadn't she said that when we got back Fallut was going to marry her?

'I bumped into a man . . .'

He fell back heavily on his pillow, and his whole face crumpled up in an expression of utter agony.

'Since you know . . .' he croaked.

'Yes. It was Jean-Marie's father. The trawler was in dock. Only the captain and Adèle were left on board. He was going to take her off. Then . . .'

'Stop! . . .'

'Then you told this man, who had come to look at the boat in which his son had died, that the kid had been murdered. Isn't that so? And you followed him! When the captain came along you hid behind a truck! . . .'

'Stop!'

'The crime was committed before your eyes . . .'

'Please!'

'No! You were a party to the crime. You went on board! And you took the woman off . . .'

'By then I didn't want her any more!'

Outside there was a loud siren blast. Le Clinche's lips trembled and he stammered:

'The *Océan* . . .'

'Yes. . . . She sails at high tide.'

They were silent. All the sounds of the hospital came to their ears, including the subdued rumble of a stretcher being wheeled towards the operating-theatre.

'I didn't want her any more! . . .' the operator repeated convulsively.

'Only it was too late . . .'

There was another silence. Then Le Clinche said:

'And yet . . . now . . . I so much want to . . .'

He didn't dare pronounce the word on his tongue.

'To live? . . .' asked Maigret.

'O, don't you understand? I was mad . . . I don't understand it myself. It all happened somewhere else, in another world. We came back here and I realized it. Listen! There was that black cabin and ourselves outside it. And nothing else existed. It seemed to be my whole life. I just wanted to hear her say *My big boy* again. I couldn't even say how it happened. I opened the door. She went away. There was a man in yellow shoes waiting for her, and they fell into each other's arms on the quay . . .

'I must have been dreaming. That is the right word for it. . . . And from that moment I wanted not to die.

... Then Marie Léonnec came with you.... Adèle came too, along with that man ...

'But what did you expect me to say? ...'

'It's too late, isn't it? ... They let me out. I went on board and got a revolver. Marie was waiting for me on the quay. She didn't know ...

'And that afternoon that woman began talking.... And there was the man with yellow shoes too ...

'Who could conceivably understand all that? ... I fired.... It took me a long time to make up my mind. ... Because Marie Léonnec was there! ...'

'Now ...'

He sobbed. He literally cried:

'I'll have to die all the same! And I don't want to die! I'm afraid to die. I ... I ...'

He began tossing about so violently that Maigret called a nurse, who, with the calm precise movements acquired during long years of professional experience, managed to quieten him.

A second time the trawler gave its piercing summons, and women ran to line up on the jetty.

11. The *Ocean* Sails

Maigret arrived at the quay just as the new captain was giving the order to cast off the hawsers. He saw the chief engineer saying good-bye to his wife, and went up and took him aside.

'Tell me something. It was you, wasn't it, who found the captain's will and put it in the police letter-box?'

The other hesitated, rather anxiously.

'You've nothing to fear. You suspected Le Clinche. You thought it was the way to save him. Although you had been after the same woman ...'

The siren shrieked angrily to late-comers, and on the quay couples loosened their embraces.

'Please don't talk to me any more about it.... Is it true he's going to die? ...'

'Unless they can save him. Where was the will?'

'In the captain's papers ...'

'And what was it you were looking for?'

'I hoped to find a photo ...' he confessed, with lowered head. 'You'll excuse me. I've got to ...'

The hawsers fell into the water. The gangway was being taken up. The chief engineer jumped on board and gave a last wave to his wife and a last look at Maigret.

Slowly the trawler made its way towards the harbour exit. A man was carrying the cabin-boy, who was scarcely fifteen, on his shoulders. The boy had taken the man's pipe and was holding it proudly between his teeth.

On shore women were crying.

By walking quickly one could follow the ship, which only got up speed when it was beyond the jetties. People shouted their last-minute instructions.

'If you meet the *Atlantique*, don't forget to tell Dugodet about his wife ...'

The sky was still overcast. The wind ruffled the sea and raised little white waves which made an angry noise.

A Parisian in flannel trousers, followed by two laughing girls in white, was taking photographs of the ship's departure.

Maigret nearly knocked down a woman who clutched his arm and asked:

'Well? ... Is he any better?'

It was Adèle. She couldn't have powdered her face since the morning, because it was quite shiny.

'Where's Buzier?' Maigret asked.

'He preferred to hop it to Le Havre. He was afraid of trouble. And, as I'd told him, I was giving him the bird ... But that boy, Pierre Le Clinche? ...'

'I don't know.'

'Tell me! ...'

But he didn't. He left her to her fate. He had caught sight of a group on the jetty: Marie Léonnec, her father, and Madame Maigret. All three were turned towards the trawler which was just passing them, and Marie Léonnec was saying fervently:

'That's *his* boat ...'

Maigret went forward slowly, grumpily. His wife was the first to see him in the crowd of people who had come to see the sailing of the Newfoundland ship.

'Have they saved him?'

Monsieur Léonnec's monstrosity of a nose turned anxiously towards him.

'Ah! I am very glad to see you. ... Where does the inquiry lead now, Inspector?'

'Nowhere!'

'You mean ... ?'

'Nothing. I don't know.'

Marie's eyes opened wide with astonishment.

'But Pierre?'

'The operation was successful. He'll probably pull through.'

'He's innocent, isn't he? ... Please. ... Tell my father he's innocent ...'

Her whole soul was in the request. And Maigret, as he looked at her, imagined how she would be in ten years' time, with the same features as her father, and rather a severe expression, meant to impress her father's customers.

'He didn't kill the captain ...' he said.

Then, turning to his wife:

'I've just had a telegram recalling me to Paris.'

'Already? I had promised to go bathing tomorrow with ...'

He gave her a look and she understood.

'You'll excuse us . . .'

'But we'll accompany you as far as the hotel . . .'

Maigret caught sight of Jean-Marie's father, dead-drunk, shaking his fist again at the trawler, and turned away his head.

'Don't trouble, please.'

'Tell me!' declared Monsieur Léonnec. 'Do you think I could take him back to Quimper? People are bound to talk.'

Marie looked pleadingly at him. She was quite pale. 'Seeing he is innocent! . . .' she stammered.

Maigret's face wore its vaguest and grimmest expression.

'I don't know. It would probably be best . . .'

'But you'll allow me to offer you something . . . a bottle of champagne? . . .'

'No, thank you.'

'A small glass. . . . How about some Benedictine, as we're in the district? . . .'

'I'll have a glass of beer.'

Upstairs, Madame Maigret was fastening up the bags.

'So you're of my opinion, are you? He's a good boy . . .'

Still that pleading look from the girl, begging him to say yes!

'I think he'll make a very good husband . . .'

'And a good business man!' The father outdid him. 'For I don't intend to let him go sailing off for many months to come. Once you're married, you've got to . . .'

'Of course!'

'Particularly as I have no son. . . . You'll understand that! . . .'

'Of course . . .'

Maigret kept looking at the stairs. Finally his wife appeared.

'The bags are ready. It seems there is no train until . . .'

'Never mind! We'll hire a car . . .'

It was a real flight!

'If you ever have the occasion to visit Quimper . . .'

'Yes. . . . Yes . . .'

Still that look from the girl. She seemed to realize that it wasn't quite so clear as it appeared, but she was begging Maigret to keep quiet.

She wanted to have her fiancé.

The inspector shook hands, paid his bill, and finished his beer.

'Thank you a thousand times, Monsieur Maigret . . .'

'Don't mention it.'

The car that had been telephoned for had arrived.

. . . and, unless you have discovered elements that have escaped me, I conclude by suggesting that this case be classified as . . .

It was a passage out of a letter from Superintendent Grenier, of the Le Harvre *Brigade Mobile*, to which Maigret replied by wire:

AGREED.

Six months later he received a communication which read:

Madame Veuve Le Clinche has the honour of announcing the marriage of her son Pierre to Mademoiselle Marie Léonnec . . . etc. . . . etc. . . .

And, a little later, when he was on a case that necessitated visiting a special house in the Rue Pasquier, he thought he recognized a young woman who turned her head away.

It was Adèle.

That was all! Except that, five years later, Maigret passed through Quimper. He saw a rope merchant standing at his shop door. He was quite a young man, very tall, but with the beginnings of a paunch.

He had a slight limp. He was calling to a little boy of three who was playing with a top on the pavement.

'Better come in, Pierrot! Mamma will be cross!'

The man, preoccupied with his offspring, did not see Maigret, who, moreover, hurried past, looking the other way and making a rather rueful face.